MARTHA, MARTHA!

By

MARGE GREEN

"... *Martha, Martha, thou art careful and troubled about many things; but one thing is needful: and Mary hath chosen that good part* ...."

—LUKE 10:38-42

QUALITY PUBLICATIONS
P.O. BOX 7385
FT. WORTH, TX 76111
1-800-359-7708

This work is dedicated to three women.

These three have truly exemplified the spirit of Mary, in seeking the "good part" and have influenced my life greatly.

TO MYRTLE THOMPSON

who was the first person to influence me to serve.

To Jo BASS

whose influence has helped me better live the Christian life.

To HELEN BASS

who gave birth to me and who daily gives her time so that I may be free to serve in other ways.

TABLE OF CONTENTS

FOREWORD

The day was Friday. The week was drawing to its end, and so were the nerves of the young mother. The days before had been especially hectic. On Monday, there had been the regular meeting of her Girl Scout troup; on Tuesday, a coffee meeting of her PTA committee. She was busy on Wednesday with a district Scout meeting and Thursday she taught the weekly ladies' class. Now Friday was upon her and she felt taut and nervous.

Everything had seemed to go wrong and she was taking her feelings out on her family. Harsh words sent the children off to school while she stooped to clean up the spilled cereal the baby had knocked over. Her husband came in to kiss her goodbye but she did not feel like being affectionate. With more unkind words the gentle husband was sent to work. In a few minutes she heard the door close and then the sound of the car motor came to her. She sat back on the floor, already tired and the day had just begun!

She picked up the baby, wiped her face and placed her in the play pen. "I'd better comb my hair and brush my teeth before I start any work" she thought. Walking into the bedroom, she looked at herself in the mirror. What was this? There in a corner of the mirror was a sheet of paper and on it in her husband's handwriting were two words—"Martha, Martha!"

Her tired mind could not comprehend the meaning. "Why, *my* name isn't Martha." Then down in the corner she saw he had written, "Read Luke 10: 38-42." On the bedside table lay the Bible she used to read each night before retiring—before she got so busy. She took it and turned to the passage.

"Now it came to pass, as they went, that he entered into a certain village: and a certain woman named Martha received him into her house. And she had a sister called Mary, which also sat at Jesus' feet, and heard his word. But Martha was cumbered about much serving, and came to him, and said, Lord, dost thou not care that my sister hath left me to serve alone? Bid her therefore that she help me. And Jesus answered and said unto her, Martha, Martha, thou art careful and troubled about many things; But one thing is needful: and Mary hath chosen that good part, which shall not be taken away from her."

"Martha, Martha!" The two words kept repeating in her mind. As tears welled to her eyes, she knelt by the bed. How grateful she was for those words written such a long time ago! How thankful she felt for the mate who knew just where to send her for the admonition she so sorely needed! She knew she had become "troubled about many things" and she had allowed this to affect her relations with those nearest and dearest to her. Her words poured out to God and courage flowed into her heart. She had not chosen the "good part" but now, with God's help she would do just that!

Her realistic problems are typical of so many of us women in the church today. No matter what our real names, we could well be called "Martha." This gentle admonition of Christ was written for our learning—time and again we would stand in need of such chiding. As I look at myself and at my Christian sisters, it is more and more evident that too many of us have become "Marthas." Too many of us have let the cares of life take us away from the better part. We need to come back to His word to learn more of this "good part" which Mary so wisely chose.

My mind goes back through time to the day in which Christ spoke these words of wisdom. I see an ordinary household, not wealthy but perhaps even poorer than many. There are preparations under way for a meal, a company meal. For Christ, the Messiah, is coming to this house today! I see the visitor as he is ushered into the home; as he is seated and as he begins to talk with those about him. There is something magnetic about this man's speech. The words spoken seem to the listener to be the very thing he needed to hear. Such kindness and such love are woven into everyday words. To one of the women in the household, these words come to a full heart. She has never heard such wisdom in all her life. She feels compelled to come and sit at the visitor's feet as he speaks of his Father and of the love He had for all men.

In another part of the house, I see another woman, She is busy and hurried. The meal must be done just right and it must be on time. Where is that sister of hers? The sound of voices attracts her and going into the other room she sees her sister, sitting and listening with rapt attention to their visitor. Pettishly, she feels that she has been wronged. Why, here is all this work to be done and there she sits. Crossly, and hoping for sympathy, she complains to the visitor about the laziness of his listener. The words which he speaks to her are not what she expected! But they are words of wisdom which she will never forget. —

"Martha, Martha!" The sound of her name was to live in her heart forever. She knew the Master Teacher had chided for being so fretful about the problems of everyday life, but she had only gratitude for Him. Later as she was to think over and over on His words, she knew He was right and how much she had needed them.

Our needs today are for just such a gentle admonition, lest we, like Martha of old, become so involved in the daily routine of living that we forget the better part. God has been good to me in giving so generously of many blessings, among which has been the opportunity to teach several classes for women and young girls. From these classes I have learned much—more in fact, I am sure, than any who sat in them. I have seen woman in practically every role she might play in life and have experienced many of them myself. I do not stand as a judge in this work; I am neither authorized nor equipped for this. I prayerfully hope that each chapter will serve as a gentle admonition and might let you see yourself just a little clearer and in turn might give you a loving boost on your way to seeking the better part.

Much thought, time, concern, study, prayer, hope and love have gone into the preparation of this work. I can only pray you will accept it in the spirit in which it was written.

Marge Green

CHAPTER I

THE WOMAN

And God saw that it was good! His earth, His heavens, His sun, His moon — He beheld them and saw that they were good. He spoke into being the plants and the trees and He saw that they were right. Each day He continued to create and as He looked upon His work, He knew that it was perfect. He spoke to His Son, saying "Let us make man in our image." And from the dust man was fashioned. This was the creature to whom God would give His blessing so in His own image, He breathed life into Adam and he became a living soul!

The sixth day was drawing to a close and God surveyed all His labor. The beauty of nature at its most perfect stretched before Him. Into this paradise He placed Adam, for it was to be his job to dress and keep the garden of Eden. All seemed complete for Adam had finished naming all the living creatures brought before him by God. Yet all was not accomplished — there was something lacking. "And the Lord God said, It is not good that the man should be alone; I will make an helpmeet for him" (Genesis 2:18). And it was thus that woman came into being.

Milton's words in *Paradise Lost* catch just a glimpse of the beauty of this creation.

> "*Under His forming hands a creature grew,*
> *Man like, but different sex; so lovely fair,*
> *That what seemed fair in all the world, seemed now*
> *Mean, or in her summed up, in her contained,*
> *and in her looks: . . .*
> *Grace was in all her steps, heaven in her eye,*
> *In every gesture dignity and love.*"

Everything which God created was good. We are told this in His own words. Yet there is only one creation for which He saw a specific need and created just to fulfill that need. This is the blessing He passed to woman. God saw all that He had done and that it was good. Yet He saw there was a need for something else, and that was woman. How humble this should make every female since she, and she alone, was created because God saw the necessity for it. What a place of honor woman was given and in truth, it might be said that she was the crowning glory of God's work. Man was to be the head of all creation but woman was given the opportunity to be the crown for that head.

Not only was woman created to fill a specific need but she was made from finer material than that of man. Adam was formed from the dust of the earth but God did not choose the dust to produce his mate. She was made from part of Adam's body. "Why?" we ask. By searching the word of God, we can get at least some reasons for this though the complete truth may never be ours until that first day of Eternity when we shall know all. First, woman was formed from man to show her unity with him as part of himself. When a man and woman are married, God says they become "one flesh." This can be more literally seen when we realize we were fashioned from a physical part of man, and not from some unrelated material.

Because she was made from him, woman has a right to man's love and protection. God did not want Adam to be alone so He fashioned woman and brought her to him. All things were in readiness for this being; a husband, a home, a purpose. Because she was "bone of his bone and flesh of his flesh" Adam knew he must love her. He did not have to be told this for when God presented woman to him, he knew that she was a part of him and therefore deserved his care and allegiance.

In the New Testament (Acts 17:26) Luke testifies that from one blood or flesh God created all mankind. This, too, would give an added reason for woman to be made from man instead of dust. God created Adam full grown and from Adam He created woman, also full grown. Their propagation from this time forward was to be according to the law of God set forth that each should reproduce in its own seed after its own kind. This gives absolutely no comfort to those who try to make us believe that humanity evolved. For in the first human beings, we see one created full grown from another. Certainly no hint of evolving could come from this. God created Adam and all mankind came from this one flesh, or blood.

When Adam awoke and saw the being which God gave to him, he called her Woman. Literally, this means "from man" or in some translations, "womb-man." Her creation signified the closeness of these two for as one ancient philosopher wrote, "She was made of a rib taken from his side — not made out of his head, to rule over him; nor out of his feet, to be trampled on by him; but out of his side, to be equal with him; under his arm, to be protected; and near his heart, to be loved." No more accurate description of her position has ever been penned.

Her name in the beginning was simply Woman. She was given to Adam and they lived together in the perfection of Eden. Though taken from man, her position was not inferior to his. One writer has stated, "Where there is no sin, there is no inequality." God created woman, not inferior to man, but equal to him. The need as God saw it was for a helpmeet for man. Modern translation seems to have changed this to *helpmate* and of course, woman should be just this. But the meaning of *helpmeet* is different. God looked at all the animals He had created and while He saw that they were good, there was nothing suitable to be the companion for Adam. Woman was created as a help "suitable" for man — suitable in that she fitted his needs physically and emotionally.

Her position was equal in level of importance with Adam's but the sphere in which she was to move was different. God did not intend for woman to be degraded or lowered to slavery. There was a place for her to fill just as Adam had his position or sphere of life. And as long as sin was not in the world, Adam and his wife lived in peace, harmony, love and joy. They walked in communion with God, each one filling the place for which he was created.

But we see almost immediately in the story of their life this perfect situation was not to last. For God had given both man and woman the ability to think and choose their way of living. He had given them one simple law, "Do not eat of the tree of the knowledge of good and evil." And the punishment for breaking this law? "For in the day that thou eatest thereof thou shalt surely die" (Genesis 2:17).

And now we begin to see some of the characteristics with which God endowed woman when He created her. For when temptation came to humanity, it came first to the female. God's account of this scene describes the serpent as more subtle than any animal He had made. Using this wily craftiness, he rightly approached the woman instead of Adam. So it would seem that woman was to be more easily tempted than man. She became a *rationalizer* at that moment in the garden and she has continued in this capacity down through the intervening ages of time.

God had said, "Ye shall surely die." But the serpent said, "Ye shall *not* surely die." We can also see the mind of woman as she began to ponder this decision she was facing. She looked at the fruit and it appealed to her; it was good for food and she was hungry. And if she ate of it, she would become wise! Her thoughts might have been something like this — "See how beautiful this fruit is? Certainly God would not want to be withholding something good from us." Or perhaps, "If we become wise like God, we can do a lot of good." But strongest of all must have been the thought that God would not make them suffer the consequences of just eating this fruit. The serpent must undoubtedly be right; they would *not* surely die. She had rationalized herself into believing that she could disobey God and still not have to pay the penalty! With this false sense of security, woman made the first mistake of her life. She believed a lie and she ate of the fruit. This act of disobedience brought sin into the world. As women we cannot pass the blame to man. True, she gave to Adam and he did eat also, but as women, we must face the ugly truth that it was his wife that took the action which released the terribleness of sin. Hers is the responsibility and nothing releases her from this guilt.

How sad it is as we look at the woman now. From a state of perfection, her foolishness had brought her and her husband to be separated from God. If we had to go off and leave womankind at this point, there would be no comfort at all for us as her descendants. She had sinned; she had caused her husband to sin; and they were separated from God. But just as God had loved His creatures in the beginning, He loved them still. They must pay the penalty for disobedience of His law, but, even now in His infinite grace He wanted to comfort them with the balm of a promise with a distant fulfillment, that a Redeemer for sin would come.

In Genesis 3:14-19 God pronounces the penalties for breaking His law. From this time forward woman was to bear children in pain, and sorrow was to come upon her. She was now to be in subjection to man and he was to have the rule over her. Her husband would have to work hard for just the food they were to eat and this job would be made more difficult by the thorns and thistles that were now to infest the fields.

The most terrifying punishment of all was then pronounced upon them. They would start dying as of that time. Their bodies would begin to decay and this eventually would take the physical part of them back to dust of the earth. Death had come into the world! How woman must have berated herself! Why did she listen to the serpent? Why did she disobey God? Her heart must have been filled with sorrow and shame at the results of her misdeed. But God said something that made the load a little easier to bear. She lifted her head and listened.

"I will put enmity between thee and the woman, and between thy seed and her seed; it shall bruise thy head, and thou shall bruise his heel" (Genesis 3:15). God was promising that in some future year one of her descendants would be used to bring a Redeemer into the world! The seed of woman was to deal a death blow to Satan! In the days and years to come, this thought was to give the only comfort woman was to know in the sorrow of the life she had made for herself. With this new life she was given a new name for Adam now called her Eve, because she was to be the mother of all living.

The picture Eve presents as a woman is an accurate study in the position, ability, character and personality of womankind as a whole. Centuries have passed but the basic nature of the female is still the same. Her clothing may have changed, her moral values been affected by customs of the day; but still woman remains the same in character and behavior. She can change her make-up; she can change her position in life but she cannot change what God gave woman in the beginning.

GOD GAVE WOMAN THE ABILITY TO BE SUITABLE FOR MAN'S NEED. In His wisdom God created woman the physical being she is. In the natural course of life, she is the only thing suited to man's physical needs. The female body is a marvelous creation, molded and fashioned by God for specific purposes. When we think upon the miracle that is our physical body we feel as the Psalmist did when he wrote, "I will praise thee; for I am fearfully and wonderfully made: marvelous are thy works; and that my soul knoweth right well" (Psalms 139:14).

The female body was created differently than the male. She is softer, more rounded. The contours were fashioned for specific needs, for in fulfilling the life which God meant woman to lead, her body plays a most important part. If we keep our bodies clean and clothed as commanded in God's word, then there is no need for shame as to how we are made. In the beginning the man and his wife were naked and were not ashamed. Only when sin came into existence did shame follow. When man and woman live in the sight of God according to His purposes, there is nothing vile nor shameful about the physical body.

GOD GAVE WOMAN THE PRIVILEGE OF BEING A MOTHER. The most sobering and wonderful blessing given woman is that of bearing children. To nothing or to no one else has He accorded the privilege of bringing a living soul into the world. The wonderfully made body of woman is geared specifically to produce this baby — from the conception of the tiny seed, through the nurturing of its growth and finally to the moment of birth. Man is necessary to this process but it is to woman that God endowed the precious power to give birth to the miracle that mankind and all his science can never reproduce — life.

GOD GAVE WOMAN THE RESPONSIBILITY OF SERVING OTHERS. Because of the very character of woman, she is more fitted to serve others. Her nature is more sympathetic; her touch is more gentle and comforting. Her voice is pitched normally to be pleasing in dealing with the problems of others. She was created to suit and serve man — not as a slave — but as a servant of love. Her first fulfillment as a mother enriches this life of service. She is made to care for the babe and the toddler with the touch of love that means security for them.

As woman matures in years she has the experience with which to better serve those around her. A sick neighbor feels her kind and sympathetic deeds. The elderly hear her soft step as she helps with their care. The widows, the orphans, the destitute, the lonely — all can be reached by the gentleness of woman. She is admirably suited by God to fill this need.

GOD GAVE WOMAN THE HOME AS HER DOMAIN. Man can go out, and in his battle of life, might conquer great nations. He may rise to the heights of power. The world can be his, if he tries hard enough. But to woman, God has given the most valuable domain of all. He chose to let her build the very foundation stone of civilization — the home. She is especially fitted to make a room more pleasant to look at. Her nature suits her to prepare the nourishment which sustains her family. She cleans, sews, cooks, washes and irons because God knew this is her sphere of life. This is where she could excel. She has no reason to fear any usurper for she is safe and secure in the warmth of what she builds with her own abilities and hard work.

GOD GAVE WOMAN THE POWER TO INFLUENCE. We can see the powerful influence of woman in the fall of man. Adam knew God had forbidden this fruit to them yet he allowed the woman he loved to lead him into sin. And woman has been using her influence ever since. The influence which God gives each of us is neutral within itself. What we make of it determines its character. History, both divine and secular, records the good and the evil which woman's influence has brought about. Wars have been won and lost — marriages made and broken — happiness gained and lost — all through the influence of a woman. It can be the influence of a wife, a mother, a grandmother, a teacher, a sweetheart, but it is powerful. And if it is not wielded lovingly and correctly, it can bring about the damnation of the soul.

Woman was created pure, lovely, and perfect. God intended her to remain that way. He gave her a sphere of life and influence she was especially suited for, but she chose to go another way. This brought sorrow and pain to Eve and it will bring the same to us today. We of the Twentieth Century are very little different from Adam's wife. True, we wear different clothing, our hair is fixed another way and the world we live in revolves at a faster pace. But we remain basically the same as our sister in the creation.

It is not necessary for us to learn by our own experience. We can comprehend right and wrong from the mistakes of others. Eve presents to us the challenge of accepting her failure as our schoolteacher. We do not have to disobey and suffer the consequences before we can understand what God wants us to do. We can never return to the perfection of Eden, but we can order our lives by the example set forth to us by Eve and by the other women of the Bible.

SPECIAL ASSIGNMENTS

1. Have someone prepare a short report on the creation of woman from the writings of Thomas Aquinas, Augustine, or some other ancient writer. These may readily be found in any public library.

2. Have another prepare a list of characteristics which Eve possessed and find other women in the Bible who show some of these same qualities.

3. Have the class bring pictures cut out of magazines showing the different ways in which women are suited to serve. These pictures can be passed on to the teachers of the primary and beginners classes for their class use.

STOP AND THINK

1. In the light of Acts 17:26 why do you feel God made woman from a part of Adam, rather than from the dust?

2. In what ways was woman suited to Adam's needs?

3. How can woman be the "crown" to man's head if she is not to rule over him?

4. When God said a husband and wife were to be one flesh, was this speaking solely of the unity of their physical bodies?

5. How could the woman rationalize herself into believing the serpent's lie? Discuss some of the things she might have said to herself.

6. Why do you think woman is more easily tempted than man?

7. Since sin came into the world because of woman's action, how did God give her the opportunity to "redeem" her sex in the future?

8. Why should the penalty of death be the most severe of the punishments meted out?

9. Name some of the ways in which modern day womankind differs from Eve.

10. In the light of God's word, what should be our attitude toward the physical relationship of the male and female?

CHAPTER II

THE WIFE AND THE HOMEMAKER

The aisle seemed so long! She could feel the gaze of all those present. Her mind was full and so was her heart. Here she was at that point in her life she had dreamed of and wished for. She touched the beautiful white dress her mother had so lovingly stitched. She looked at the bouquet she held in her hands. All around her were the evidences of love — the love of her parents in providing this wonderful moment for her.

She lifted her eyes to the man who was walking with her, taking her down this aisle to place her life in the hands of another, younger man. This was her father, the one who had worked so hard in giving her a good life. There toward the front of the church sat her mother. She was smiling, but it was a smile mixed with both joy and sorrow. Her daughter was getting married.

Waiting at the end of the aisle stood the one with whom she had chosen to spend the rest of her life. Their eyes met with the assurance of mutual love and as she came to him, he reached out and took her hand. "Dearly Beloved," the minister began the ceremony. The words touched her heart as she tried to remember each thing said, each vow she took. "And now I pronounce you husband and wife!" He reached down and gave her a tender kiss. She placed her hand on his arm and together they turned to walk back down the aisle toward the new life they faced. They were married; they were two flesh which in the sight of God now were one.

How wonderful it would be if we could solve all the problems which lay ahead by giving this a fairy tale ending, "And they lived happily ever after!" But life is not a fairy tale and its problems are not so easily conquered. Life is living a twenty-four hour day, sometimes against seemingly overwhelming odds. And the problems of living are solved, not by looking the other way and ignoring them, but by courageously facing them. One by one, they can be met and conquered. If we try to take them on en masse, we can only bow in misery and almost certain defeat. Whatever way we choose to meet our problems, the only sure and comforting aid can be found in God. Without Him, we cannot hope to solve the issues of life, either one at a time or en masse.

Marriage is a God-given institution and the role of wife was the first placed upon woman. "And the rib which the Lord God had taken from man, made he a woman, and brought her unto the man" (Genesis 2:22). It was God who gave the first woman in marriage and in taking this step He brought upon the earth the relationship that was to mean more to mankind than any other. He took one incomplete being and placed her with another. Together they would find completeness. "What therefore God hath joined together, let not man put asunder" (Mark 10:9). God had placed them together and man was not to interfere.

Marriage is a beautiful union and true happiness can be found within it. Yet the courts of America are full of marriages being torn asunder and destroyed completely. At the time of this writing, national statistics show that two out of every five marriages will end in divorce. And when the marriages are between those in their teenage years, the ratio rises to one out of every two! Therefore it is very easy to see that though marriage is "made in heaven" it is not a divine institution. It is lived out here on earth with two human beings as the central characters. And it is up to those two to determine the course they want their marriage to take and then decide that, with God's help and guidance, they will reach the goal of earthly happiness.

Since God instituted marriage for the beings He had created, we must look to His word to find the reasons for putting man and woman together in this relationship. In Genesis 2:18 God gives the first motive. "And the Lord God said, It is not good that man should be alone; I will make him an helpmeet for him." No average, normal human being is made to live alone. Regardless of what position we might have in life, what material possessions we have, what talents we might be blessed with, a person is not completely happy if he does not have someone who is a very dear part of himself. There seems always to be a restlessness, a seeking after something. God recognized that we would have this need of companionship and He gave us marriage to fulfill it in its most complete sense.

Our natural appetites are also God-given. He instilled within each of us the need for food, drink, rest and intellectual curiosity. Each of these appetites is normal and is to be fulfilled in the God-approved way. With each appetite, He supplied an acceptable way to satisfy it. He also made us male and female and placed within us certain natural appetites of passion. Since we recognize that He gave us this appetite, then we must also accept that He has given us the approved way in which to fulfill it. God has arranged it where our desires can be satisfied legitimately, scripturally and morally in the estate of marriage.

"Marriage is honorable in all, and the bed undefiled" (Hebrews 13:4). Passion is not a dirty word. In the beginning God endowed each human with this beautiful desire and as long as it was kept within the bounds of His approval, it remained pure and holy. Only when man has taken it and placed it in surroundings and relationships other than God-sanctioned, does passion become filthy and immoral. Marriage is to provide the satisfaction of the natural appetites of the flesh.

In addition to the need of companionship and the fulfillment of our normal God-given desires, there is a third reason for marriage. God told Adam and Eve to be fruitful and multiply. He had created both of them full grown but they were to bring forth others of their kind (or multiply themselves) by the natural law of procreation which God had set in motion after the creation. Therefore marriage has the additional purpose of procreation, bringing children into the world.

"Take ye wives, and beget sons and daughters; and take wives for your sons and give your daughters to husbands, that they may bear sons and daughters; that ye may be increased there, and not diminished" (Jeremiah 29:6). God has always approved the begetting of children and has written much concerning their education and welfare. This will be covered in another chapter, however.

We have found that marriage is good and that it is approved by God. We have seen that the threefold purpose of marriage is (1) for companionship, (2) for the fulfillment of our God-given desires and (3) for the procreation of the human race. These give the general picture of marriage and are worthy of our consideration. Yet as women, we must be concerned with the role that we play in this institution. We want to see the blessings that come from the proper attitudes and actions and yes, we will even look at the sorrow and pain which will come if we stray from God's way in our role as wife.

WHAT WILL WE TAKE TO OUR MARRIAGE? Every young girl starts preparing for her marriage at a very early age. She doesn't play with hammers, guns, swords or tools. No, she plays with dishes, dolls, baby carriages and doll clothes. She is beginning even at this age to prepare for what she will become later in life. For we can tell almost with a certainty what kind of wife we will be by what kind of daughter we have been! If we are lazy and slothful in our ways, then we will take that with us when we marry. If we hate to cook and do other housework, we should not expect to be filled with joy over these tasks when we have a home of our own. We will take with us to our marriage the kind of social being we are, which will determine what kind of companions we seek. Sister T. B. Thompson has a beautiful and tender lesson which she presents to young Christian girls on "What Shall I Take to My Wedding?" I have heard this and wish fervently every teenage girl (and boy, too) could hear it and take it to heart. Aunt Myrtle says, "Each of you will take to your wedding the sum total of the person you are, and what you take will mean more to your happiness socially, and to your everlasting happiness spiritually, than any one thing in this world that you do."

Most marriages today are built on the timeworn, but still popular method of courtship. We see the young man gallantly seeking the hand of the girl he has chosen. He compliments her; he often gives her small gifts. She makes him wait for her and he is willing to do this without complaint. He opens the car door for her, helps her on with her coat, picks up things which she drops. Tenderly and solicitously he pays court to her. Truly, she sits upon the throne of his heart. She accepts his hand and they are married.

This ceremony seems to mark the beginning of change in their lives. As time goes by he gets busy and forgets the flattery he once gave. The money must support two now and there are no more small gifts. She becomes more careless and doesn't spend much time in fixing herself to look nice when he comes home from work. He doesn't compliment her much any more, but then she doesn't do much to deserve it.

Is this the marriage they both looked forward to so eagerly? Why didn't the honeymoon last? Where is the harmony they had before they said "I do?" From the standpoint of the world, this is the same story told in countless divorce courts the country over. But from the standpoint of the Christian, we must look deeper to find the causes and then go to God's word for the remedy. Because we realize that "What God hath joined together, let not man put asunder," we must not take our problems to the divorce court. We must seek counsel from God. Most problems stem from one of the partners not being willing to adjust to the situation. Harmony can only come when each is willing to put self in second place and consider the other first.

I once heard a marriage counselor state that marriage must not be the "fifty-fifty" proposition which most people think it should be. She stated that it should be a "ninety-ten" agreement. Each person should be prepared to give up his own desires ninety per cent of the time and be willing to have his own ten per cent of the time. If each partner feels this way, then harmony can prevail and the adjustments of marriage can be made.

So many young brides have the storybook idea of life. They feel that their own true love will come along. They will immediately recognize him. He will carry them away to his castle and set them upon a pedestal and there they will be adored and cared for the rest of their lives. That is just what this is — a storybook life. For in reality, we see only too well that this is not the case.

We might not even know our "true love" is around until he has been there several years. Why, we might not even like him when we meet him. Cases of love at first sight are rare indeed! He might carry us away but most of us will not be taken to a castle and what we are put upon will most certainly not be a marble pedestal. For the honeymoon will soon be over and we must get down to the normal routine of living. And this does not include a great amount of being gazed upon and adored from a pedestal. We must be busy with the day-to-day chores of making the beds, preparing the meals, doing the wash, ironing the clothes, and stretching the budget to cover three meals a day. Marriage is not a storybook affair; it is the every-day task of living with another person and trying to make our lives as harmonious and loving as we can. We must be realistic in our approach to being a wife because certainly life is realistic and can be coped with only on a down-to-earth level. God does not intend for us to live in the dream-like world of the honeymoon. We must come down to the realities of life as it actually is.

It is at man's side that woman finds her greatest degree of usefulness; her sphere of service here is superior to any other she might choose. The home is the realm given to the wife and here it is her responsibility to function as God would have her to. She is to be governed by the standards God has set forth for her.

THE WIFE MUST LOVE AND RESPECT HER HUSBAND. The very basis for any marriage must be love. The world has taken this word and twisted it to mean many things — most of them foreign to the meaning God has for it. God has commanded woman to love her husband, the Bible is full of examples of wives who did this. "And the wife see that she reverence her husband" (Ephesians 5:33). In the word *reverence* we see the fuller meaning of love, a love based not only on desire but on respect for the obedience of this person.

A woman who does not respect her husband cannot love him perfectly. There is something lacking in their relationship. She is the weaker vessel and if he does not take his place as the stronger partner, she loses respect for him. She must be willing to accept him for what he is, respecting his personality, his talents, his faults. If she married him thinking to change him, her purpose was faulty. Love accepts the person as he is, not for what we might think we can make of him. Certainly the wife should do all within her power to change the bad into good, but this must be done in perfect respect of her mate and not in a demanding, superior attitude.

THE WIFE MUST BE SUBJECT TO HER HUSBAND. This causes more grief to modern woman than perhaps any other command. In trying to get "equal" rights with man, we tend to feel that we do not have to be in subjection to anyone. Yet, God knew that we were not equipped to lead our lives this way. "Wives, submit yourselves unto your own husbands, as it is fit in the Lord" (Colossians 3:18). "Likewise, ye wives, be in subjection to your own husbands" (I Peter 3:1).

The words are plain and simple. They can be understood without long, philosophical examinations. Man is the head of the woman; she must be in subjection to him. This is God's pattern for the government of the home. When we fight against it, we can only expect to bring in heartache and trouble. Modernism, with its deceptive logic, has crept into the church, finding a too receptive welcome in many women. We do not want to be subject to anyone; we want to feel that we are just as good as the man. What woman fails to recognize is that she is not inferior to man by being subject to him. God has placed her in a position of honor in giving man the charge to take care of her as the weaker vessel. We are to be loved, protected and cherished because of the role we were placed in by God. Why should we want to throw off this mantle of protective love which God has so carefully bestowed upon us?

The question arises in such a discussion, "What if my husband is not a Christian? Do I still have to obey him?" Your relationship to your non-Christian husband is no different than your sister's who has a Christian mate. God's place for the woman is the same, no matter what her husband is religiously. The only exception would be when the husband's specific demands go against God's word. Colossians 3:18 says "as it is fit *in* the Lord." We must submit ourselves to our husbands as long as they do not ask of us anything contrary to God's way. We are told that by our subjection in meek and chaste behavior, it is possible to win our mates to the Lord (I Peter 3:1).

THE WIFE MUST LIVE IN SUCH A WAY AS TO DESERVE RESPECT. God has ably endowed woman to present to the world a life that commands respect. She is made to be feminine and that is her place in life. Femininity has become almost a bad word in our language because of the misuse mankind has given it. It is good for the woman to be feminine; man likes her that way. It is the characteristic she possesses to make him feel like the stronger vessel.

Peter tells the Christian woman to adorn herself with the inward ornaments of a meek and quiet spirit (I Peter 3:4) but God also gives us instructions as to our outward adornment (I Timothy 2:9-10). We should dress in feminine, becoming apparel, making certain the clothing is modest. Immodest apparel cannot merit womankind the respect God wishes her to have.

Woman's voice is normally keyed to be softer and more pleasant-sounding than the male's. Notice, we said *normally*. We should cultivate the kind delicate speech which makes us more feminine. Modern woman has allowed herself to become loud and harsh. Yet it has been proven time and time again that it is the soft word that is listened to and not the loud, strident voice. One of the most important things we can each our young girls is to cultivate a soft, gentle voice. This will carry more weight in any discussion than the hard argumentative speech.

Not only must we make certain our voices are kind and soft but we must be on guard against the unfeminine, vulgar speech so common today. There is not a man who will respect a woman who constantly indulges in telling the "dirty" story and in using profanity. These traits are not becoming to anyone and least of all, to the female.

THE WIFE MUST STRIVE FOR ONENESS IN MARRIAGE. When God said that man and woman were to be "one flesh" He was speaking of their relationship as a whole. And yet, this oneness is achieved most completely in the physical part of the marriage. Because these desires are normal and God-given, He has made certain that we have direct teaching concerning this relationship. The passage of I Corinthians 7:2-5 gives us this specific instruction. This side of marriage is beautiful and pure and designed to fulfill man's natural appetite. It is shameful indeed when so many wives do not understand this portion of their marriage. We seem to feel there are separate standards for the male and the female but in God's sight, we must have harmony between each for the contentment to be complete.

Positive teaching should be given our young women so as to prepare them for this part of their love. There should be no feeling of guilt for this is a God-sanctioned desire. The modern world has made much of "sex" and this has colored the thinking of many women. The wife must enter this relationship with the proper attitude of love and of course, perfect love means giving. She should put the desire and satisfaction of her husband above her own considerations. And he, in turn, should be kind and understanding with her.

Spiritual love in a marriage has its beginning in this physical love. Unless this physical side is accomplished with mutual love and understanding, the more perfect spiritual love cannot bud and blossom. It should be the desire of every Christian mother to make certain her daughter has been taught the proper attitude toward, and respect for, this oneness which comes with marriage. This would mean a great step forward in making more marriages work as God desires they should.

WHEN A WOMAN BECOMES A WIFE, SHE BECOMES A HOME-MAKER. Marriage and housework go together. They are a unit and cannot be separated. When we marry the man of our choice, we automatically accept the responsibility of making a home for him and for the family we might have. This is a reality we must face. As we stated above, the honeymoon does not last but we must soon come to the task of making a home. Homemaking is the noblest occupation in the world and no woman should be ashamed to state this. This is where God placed her; this is where she can excel; this is her place of superiority.

It is impossible to speak of homemaking without getting into the physical side of it. The more spiritual level of homemaking can only come after the physical side has been accomplished to a satisfactory degree. And the physical side of keeping house involves work — good, hard, honest work. And perhaps this is what makes it distasteful to so many of us. It means we must make the beds, squeeze the orange juice, mop the floor, prepare the meals, wash and iron the clothes and countless other jobs too numerous to list.

These things must be done but it is the attitude with which we tackle them that either makes a drudgery or a labor of love. Do we think of doing the dishes as merely cleaning up a mess? If we would look at it as serving those we love best, it puts a different light on the job. After all, if we have the attitude that we *have* to do these things, it will seem repellent to us. Aren't we fortunate to have the opportunity to *get* to do this? Wouldn't it be awful if we were not needed by anyone?

In a recent article on marriage problems, a columnist wrote, "Women don't keep their husbands because they don't keep their houses." Husbands come home from the tense atmosphere of the business world to a house full of similar tension. The basis of homemaking is keeping the house physically clean. We do not have to be slaves to our homes, but we must do everything possible to see that our home is bright, tidy and cheerful and that our disposition matches it. The home should be a place of peace and harmony, a rest from the dog-eat-dog business world. When our husband comes home from work, we should see that the housework is done and that we present to him a picture of neatness, ready to be a companion to him. So often he walks in the door and we don't give him time to get rid of the burdens of his job before we load him down with the burden of our problems!

The wife has the responsibility to see that the home is neatly kept and tastefully furnished. It is not the cost of the furniture that is important but how it is selected and placed. Sometimes it may be necessary to use apple crates and orange boxes for furniture. If this is true, we can still see that they are neatly arranged and made just as attractive as possible. It is the living and attitudes in the house that make it into a home — not the drapes, carpeting and expensive furniture.

As much as we dislike the word *organization*, it is necessary to employ just that in being a good homemaker. Keeping a good house does not just *happen*; a lot of hard work and planning and organization is behind the smoothly running exterior presented to the world. It is well for the wife to make a schedule for her work so that she can fit in each job that needs to be done. This schedule should not be so rigid that it cannot be broken for extras that might crop up or for some small emergency that arises. But if we put a routine into our work, it will assure us of getting more done in the time available. We needn't be afraid of organization if we make it serve us instead of being a slave to it.

Being a good homemaker includes being a wise manager of the financial means available to the home. Perhaps more friction comes from this than any other thing. The wife who does not try to live within their income is foolish indeed and may very well be the cause of her husband's early death. Sociologists have proven in their studies that the man who is "pushed" into making more money is the frequent object of heart attacks and related illnesses. It is well for the wife to have ambition for the husband but to have the desire for material possessions to such an extent that it brings pressure upon the husband is not only unwise, but is not according to God's plan of being subject to our husbands. We must be willing to manage our household on what our husband makes or else make any adjustments necessary to bring our budget into line with our income. To live within his income is a precious gift every wife should give her husband.

We have spoken of some of the positive attributes of the godly wife, but there are some negatives which we should discuss. God's word contains both positive and negative commands and to study one without the other would be presenting a one-sided picture.

THE WIFE MUST NOT PUT OTHERS BEFORE HER HUSBAND. The wife and husband are the basic unit of the marriage. Any other element must fit into this relationship without disturbing the original pattern of the man as being the head and the woman as his helpmeet. The woman should not place anything or anybody above her husband. He is the primary concern of her life and she must learn to fit in children, friendships, clubs, and other activities with regard to their importance but never are they placed before him. Any activity or person which comes between husband and wife should be analyzed and quickly adjusted to its proper position in order that the God-given pattern not be distorted or destroyed.

THE WIFE SHOULD NOT BE JEALOUS. In the Christian marriage there can be no place for jealousy. Indeed, there is no place for it because there is no reason for it. The husband who trusts in his wife need have no fear that she will betray that trust. The wife who loves her husband does not concern herself about being jealous of his words or deeds. She knows that he loves her as he loves himself and therefore will not hurt her. Jealousy can only bring disunity and confusion and unhappiness and should have no place in the Christian home. Proper trust is based on having the proper love for one another. If this exists, there can be no jealousy.

THE WIFE MUST NOT BE A NAGGING, CONTENTIOUS WOMAN. Husbands are driven into the comforting arms of others by the constant fussing, contention and strife caused by a nagging wife. It has been said that the only thing God left Job was a nagging wife and he would have been better off without her. The wisdom of the Proverbs tells us of the ugliness of a contentious woman. "It is better to dwell in the corner of a housetop, than with a brawling woman in a wide house" (Proverbs 25:24). "The contentions of a wife are a continual dropping" (Proverbs 19:13). In other words, the nagging wife gets on the nerves like a constantly dripping faucet!

The story of Samson shows that woman can get her way by constant nagging but that it seldom, if ever, brings her happiness. Delilah wanted to know Samson's secret and she kept after him. At first he was amused at her coaxing and begging but it kept up until it became nagging. "And it came to pass, when she pressed him daily with her words, and urged him, that his soul was vexed unto death" (Judges 16:16). She literally nagged him to the point of wanting to die! And she got her way. She learned his secret but the ensuing events proved how hollow was her victory. Surely we can learn from this example!

THE WIFE MUST NOT RESENT HER IN-LAWS. When a girl marries a young man, she is accepting his family as well. She must learn to be a part of them as she expects him to become a part of her own family. She should realize that the man she loves and is accepting as her husband has become what he is through the influence of his parents. She should be grateful for their care and concern that molded his personality into what she fell in love with. Resentment can have no part in the Christian wife's life. More will be studied and discussed concerning in-laws in a later chapter.

The rewards of a Christian wife and homemaker are many. Not only does she have the respect of her husband and her family, but she respects herself. The picture of the worthy woman in Proverbs 31 shows that if we attain the goal this woman did, our husband and children will praise us and call us blessed. No greater earthly reward can any woman seek than to be praised by her husband! Not only will our good life bring a fuller, richer existence here on earth but it could very well mean the salvation of our own souls, as well as that of our husband and family.

Let us search our ways; examine our goals. How are we building our house? Are we, perhaps, tearing it down? Each married woman faces this choice and Proverbs 14:1 tells us "Every wise woman buildeth her house: but the foolish plucketh it down with her hands." Are we building or destroying? The decision is ours. What shall we do? "Whoso findeth a wife findeth a good thing, and obtaineth favor of the Lord" (Proverbs 18:22). Are our husbands happy with what they have found in us?

SPECIAL ASSIGNMENTS

1. Have one member read Proverbs 31:10-31 and discuss the favorable characteristics of this worthy wife.

2. Have another member take three Bible wives (Perhaps Sarah, Rachel, Rebekah) and give a short discussion on their relationship with their husbands.

3. Have someone find a recent newspaper article about some wife — either good or bad — and discuss the blessings or problems her actions brought about.

STOP AND THINK

1. What is wrong with taking the romantic, storybook attitude toward love and marriage?

2. Why does man not have the right to "put asunder" a marriage?

3. Give the three basic purposes for marriage. What is the part that woman plays in each and what should her attitude be toward each?

4. How can we be certain that we take the right things to our marriage?

5. Why are so many young couples disillusioned after only a short period of married life? What could be done to better prepare them for the realities of married life?

6. Why is it a blessing that the "honeymoon" doesn't last forever?

7. How can our attitude toward our housework make it any easier for us?

8. Why do you feel that woman will be happier in obedience to God's command to be in subjection to her husband?

9. What is the Christian's attitude and relationship to the non-Christian mate?

10. In what ways can organization serve to make us better wives?

CHAPTER III

THE MOTHER

The photograph album lay open on her lap. As she turned the pages looking at each picture of her children, she relived the many precious years of motherhood. Time had been good to her — a good husband, lovely children and now God had blessed her with grandchildren. As the pages passed before her, she realized the changes each year had brought. How inexperienced she had been when the first baby came! How grateful she was to God for His help in guiding her through those difficult times!

She began to question herself. How did she mature as a mother? Was she a better mother with the last child than with the first? What mistakes had she made that she could have avoided if she had only used the advice and admonitions of the Bible? What pitfalls had she been able to avoid because she knew what God wanted her to do? Life had been good because God had been good! She knew her job was not finished yet because there was still much to help teach her own daughters and the young women in the church. No time to rest now; she must be up and about her "Father's business."

The word *Mother* is the softest word in our language. There is no single definition that would perfectly describe it. To tell what *Mother* is and what it means would take volumes of words put together from understanding hearts who had loving mothers. Yet even then there would be an inadequacy in all that might be written. We can only say that it is a God-given blessing bestowed upon womankind for her own well-being and for the well-being of the children she produces.

Unto woman God granted the unique and exclusive privilege of cooperating with the Creator in bringing a living soul into the world. This is as close to creation as it is humanly possible to get. Man has never yet and never will be able to duplicate or create life as God does. This is His exclusive right, but He has lovingly granted to woman an important part in exercising this right. For this she should be eternally grateful.

The importance of being a mother cannot be exaggerated. At the heart of almost every good thing is a tiny seed planted by some mother. Her deeds and words have done more to inspire man than any other thing. Abraham Lincoln said, "All that I am, or ever hope to be, I owe to my Mother." Even self-willed crusty Napoleon stated, "The destiny of the child is the work of the mother." No matter how many aeons may pass, it is a true maxim that the hand that rocks the cradle still rules the world.

When a young girl reaches her physical maturity, by the law of nature she is able to bear a child. Yet there is much more to being a mother than just having a baby. In the eyes of the world the physical act makes one a parent, but in the eyes of God it requires a great deal more. Only with God's help and daily communion with Him can we expect to meet the greatest challenge any woman faces — the incredibly simple sounding but fantastically intricate privilege of being a mother.

"Lo, children are an heritage of the Lord: and the fruit of the womb is his reward. As arrows are in the hand of a mighty man; so are the children of youth. Happy is the man that hath his quiver full of them" (Psalms 127:3-5). Perhaps only those who do not obtain the blessing of motherhood can fully understand just how great a heritage these children are. God sends them as a gift to mankind, to be loved and cherished, cared for and taught. The destiny of earthly kingdoms lies in the hands of children who will grow up in the way taught by their parents. If mothers would realize this terribly awesome certainty, perhaps there would be more active training and less passive "taking care of" our children.

An ancient Spanish proverb states, "An ounce of the mother is worth a pound of the clergy." There is much truth in this for it is the mother who has more influence in training the child than any other person. The father, the Bible school, the church, the public school — all have a part. But the first seeds of knowledge are sown in that small babe by the mother. The sad part is that too many of us seem to think we have to wait for our children to get older before we do any positive teaching.

A prominent educator once spoke to a group of mothers. After the speech one mother came up and said that she had a five year old son and then asked, "How soon should I start training him?" The educator answered, "Hurry home! You have already wasted the five most precious years!" Sad, but true. Psychologists state that the child forms his basic character in the first eight years of life. His traits and ideas are merely molded more firmly until he is eighteen. Studies have proved that few change their character after the age of eighteen! So we can see the necessity of using our time wisely as mothers before the clay of young life is hardened and can be shaped no more.

Before we begin training our children, we should first take a good look at ourselves. What kind of mother are we? Children learn best by example and they learn most from *our* example. What kind of example do we place before them? Any desire for betterment should start with a self-evaluation and this is what we shall do — look at ourselves as mothers.

Every mother has a dream, an ideal for her child. What that dream is will differ, of course, with each mother. Hannah had a dream of giving her child to God's service. Bathsheba had a dream of her son being king. But the common goal of every mother is to have her child grow up to be a competent, self-sufficient, happy person. This goal should be kept in mind constantly and applied to ourselves. We should realize that our child will probably be no better than we are — unless some strong outside influence comes to bear upon him. If we desire a better life for our children, we should always be striving to better ourselves. For as time goes by these children will be a mirror for our own attitudes, our personalities and our character. Very seldom does our offspring rise above the dreams, ambitions and ideals that we implant in them when they are young.

In the modern world woman trains herself to achieve many careers. Medicine, business, science — all these fields are open to women today. She will spend years preparing herself for her chosen work. Yet every day countless hundreds of babies are born to women who have had no training whatsoever to make them better mothers. Since being a mother is the most important career a woman can undertake, is it not reasonable to expect her to give time and thought to making herself a successful mother?

As mothers we have to live just today. We must never borrow trouble from yesterday or tomorrow. We should take every day as it comes and use each hour as a positive gift from God. If we do this, our yesterdays can be forgotten and our tomorrows will take care of themselves. The motto of motherhood should be Philippians 4:6-7, "In nothing be anxious; but in everything by prayer and supplication with thanksgiving let your requests be made known unto God. And the peace of God, which passeth all understanding, shall keep your hearts and minds through Christ Jesus." Time is the mother's most precious possession in training her children and she cannot afford to waste any of it on useless worrying. Action is the necessary thing and worry is wasted effort — negative and not needed.

THE PRIMARY STEP A MOTHER MUST TAKE IS TO BE A CHRISTIAN HERSELF. If we have not heard, believed, repented, confessed and been baptized, we have a very shaky foundation upon which to build the lives of our children. We must possess great faith. If our own faith is small, we cannot expect our child's to be greater. And most important, we must live that faith in everyday action. Our children should see that God is important to us — that He is first in our lives.

WE MUST TAKE THE PROPER ATTITUDE TOWARD GOD AND HIS CHURCH. The mother is responsible to a great extent for the spiritual attitude of the whole family. If we are anxious to serve God, this will soon become contagious with the others in the home. It is the mother who can make certain that time is allotted for home worship and Bible study. It is the mother who will prepare the family for the worship services on Sunday and during the week. If we would take a close look at our homes at those times immediately prior to going to the church building, our eyes might be opened to many mistakes we are making. Do we have a grouchy "Hurry, Hurry" attitude? If we do not get up at the right time and then have to push everyone at fever pitch, how can they go to worship or Bible study with a calm, receptive mind? We should make certain that we are prepared ahead of time so that the hour prior to worship will make our family be quiet and happy and filled with expectation of the coming study or worship. If we find that our children are dreading going to church, we should take a long hard look at what we are doing in our preparation for these events.

The mother should use the Bible as her daily guide. She must know what it contains for how can she teach if she herself does not know. It is not the duty of the Bible school class to have the sole responsibility of teaching our children. How can two or three hours a week counterbalance all the other hours spent on things of the world? We spend time on many things but just how much time do we give to teaching our children about God in our homes? Even the smallest child learns much about God in everyday things. The flower growing in the window box — did it not come from God? The food on the table — did not God provide this for us? The sun, the rain, our home, our loved ones — all are an excellent source of teaching the little ones of God.

Good Christian literature should be provided for the family. If we have nothing provided for our children to read in the way of books and magazines geared to the Christian's needs, we should not expect them to search out these things for themselves. Most young people take the easy way out by reading only what is at hand so it is most important to see that such reading matter is always at hand. And we should encourage them to delve into it.

We have a definite promise from God that if we train our children properly in His way, we have no need to fear how they will turn out. Where does God say this? Proverbs 22:6, "Train up a child in the way he should go; and when he is old, he will not depart from it." Notice the concreteness of this promise. "When he is old, he *will not* depart from it." He doesn't say *should not*, but it is a positive *will not*. The responsibility is ours as parents then to see that the way we are training our children is the way he should go, or in other words, God's way.

THE MOTHER MUST BE CONCERNED WITH THE PHYSICAL WELL-BEING OF HER CHILDREN. Luke 2:52 says that Jesus' growth included all facets of his being — the physical, the intellectual, the social, as well as the spiritual. If Mary and Joseph saw to it that Jesus was brought up properly in each of these, then we must do the same for our children. Of necessity, the first concern we have for our babies is for their physical well-being. When they are first born, they are helpless and in need of loving care. We wear ourselves out making sure that we do everything possible to protect their physical bodies. We feed them carefully. We spend hours washing and ironing the proper clothing for their soft bodies. We diligently see that everything is kept sterilized so that no germs might come in contact with them.

Yet as they grow older, we become more concerned about the other facets of their personality and sometimes we forget the importance of seeing that their bodies are well cared for. I recently read an article on teenage skin problems. This article stated that over two million dollars is spent annually for skin preparations, healing ointments, and cover-all make-up. More young girls and boys are having skin problems than at any other time in history. The experts declare that this is caused by (1) too little exercise and (2) too much of the wrong kind of food and drink. Very little of it is caused by disease or internal problems.

As mothers of these young people, we stand indicted. Do we make certain that our children receive the balanced diet they should have? Are we making certain that they get enough exercise and the right amount of sleep? So often we take the easy way out and let things slide along until the problem is almost too much to overcome. We have forgotten that our bodies are the temple of God (I Corinthians 3:16) and we have let them be defiled and perhaps even destroyed by careless habits. From a very early age we should teach our children the proper care of their bodies and this includes diet, cleanliness and exercise. To harm the body is sinful and we should help our loved ones avoid this pitfall.

THE MOTHER MUST ENCOURAGE THE GROWTH OF HER CHILD'S INTELLECT. It is usually the mother who introduces the child to the beautiful things of life. She is the one who encourages him to learn more about the special interests he might have. The child who has no knowledge of good books, music, or art is a pauper in life no matter how wealthy the home. Children have such open minds and are so receptive to learning new things. The mother should never be too busy to stop and answer any questions the child might have concerning nature, life or even the common things most children ask about, "Why this?" or "Why that?" She might not have the answer handy but together she and the child can seek the solution. It is a wise mother who early introduces her children to the library and the many wonders it holds. Through this institution she can gain much help in opening doors of learning to her children. There are recordings of fine music to be checked out. There are films which can be borrowed and shown to groups of neighborhood friends. And the world of adventure, love, science and life in general awaits on each book shelf for the eager reader to experience.

There are many ways the mother can provide intellectual stimulation for her youngsters. Most cities have museums, both of art and history, where wonderful hours can be spent. In the summers there are free band concerts and often there are theater projects for children, which charge no admission. We should not try to push our children into these avenues of learning but we can take them by the hand and lead them into the new adventures the good things of life have to offer. Before long, they will take the lead and perhaps be taking your hand to show you something exciting.

THE MOTHER MUST PROVIDE POSITIVE RECREATION FOR HER CHILDREN. There are many social activities in which Christian young people cannot participate. Yet our children want to enjoy life; they need to be part of a group and to feel accepted. We must have the courage to say "No" when what they ask to do is harmful, but we must stand ready to provide something which they can do. The young people of today are much maligned. Because of the sordid activities of a few, the majority is labeled as bad. This is not true. There are more wonderful, thoughtful and useful teenagers than there are delinquents. Most of them would rather be engaged in clean, wholesome fun than indulging in the questionable things which the world now permits and encourages them to do.

We must make certain that our homes are available for parties and other get-togethers. True, it's a little work and perhaps there will be a mess to clean up afterward. But the joy of knowing that you have given a good time to your children will more than make up for any labor you might have to do. We should *think* the best of our young people and *expect* the best of them. Then if we do our part in helping them find the righteous way, they will present their best to life.

THE MOTHER MUST TEACH HER CHILDREN RESPONSIBILITY. There is a definite trend today to overindulge our children. We give them too many privileges without the counterbalance of responsibilities. We say that we want them to become independent, self-controlled adults, yet we keep them tied to our apron strings by taking all the problems off of their shoulders. Most young people of today do not know how to work. They are not expected to do any and they very seldom take the initiative to do it on their own. We should teach our children to work and to do so joyfully. So often, we feel it is easier to do it ourselves rather than give them the responsibility. It might take them longer and perhaps it won't be as thorough a job, but they will have come a step closer to maturity.

The work you set for your child should be a challenge to him. And most often, this will be the challenge of accomplishment — the joy of a job well done. Most of us love the satisfaction of successfully completing some task. It is from this feeling of accomplishment that confidence is gained. And confidence tells us that we are needed, that we are important. We do our child no favor by handing life to him on a silver platter, shielding him from any responsibility. The failures of today can usually be traced back to a home where nothing was required *of* them but everything was done *for* them.

If our child accepts his responsibility and carries through, we should praise him. This is the best reward. Paying him to do a job about the house is not always the wisest thing. After all, this child is a part of this home and as a part, he must share in the responsibilities. Allowances are fine but they should not be given as payment for doing chores. Does mother get paid for her housework? Does daddy expect payment for painting the house or mowing the lawn? This is their responsibility to the home and the children should be taught to shoulder their share.

Teaching responsibility is not always easy. Many children will do what you ask or suggest, but the test of their training comes when little Johnny or Mary can see what has to be done and sets about doing it without being told, or nagged. This is never the answer. We should train ourselves to say something once and say it in a soft tone. Shouting never brought about anything but defiance, hurt feelings and frayed nerves. We should see that what we ask is done at once. If we tell our child to do something and then in a few minutes go do it ourselves, we have handed him an engraved invitation to avoid responsibility by doing nothing.

THE MOTHER MUST DISCIPLINE HER CHILD. Discipline for failure to obey should be as prompt as would be praise for achievement. The method of this discipline is up to the individual mother and tends to differ with each child. It might be a hickory switch, a chair in the corner, or a privilege withheld. The severity of it should be judged according to the offense. But it should never be done in anger or for self-satisfaction of the parent. Discipline without love is tyranny yet love without discipline is foolishness. The rule is "Be kind; be calm; be firm." The word *discipline* comes from the same word as disciple, which means a learner. Discipline is for guidance and teaching, and not just for punishment. The goal of our discipline is really the time when the child will have self-discipline. As the child grows up, we will not always be on hand to administer training. He must be able to see what is right and what is wrong and judge his actions accordingly. Only the disciplined child will bring delight to his parents (Proverbs 29:17).

We must make certain that we do not discipline our children negatively, or strictly for punishment. This kind is usually administered because of our failure as parents. Children should be disciplined for things that are damaging to their character rather than for an inconvenience to ourselves. Too often we administer "discipline" for some accident which could very well have happened to us. Perhaps we should ask ourselves this question when such does occur, "Is this material possession more important than the love of my child?" Then we might have the proper perspective in talking with him and not punishing him in anger.

There are times when we must come to the conclusion that we just have to accept some things. We can do nothing to change them. We should be a good sport about them. One of the most important things a mother can possess is a sense of humor and it should be kept constantly at hand. We need it so often and it proves a most valuable asset. Don't be ashamed to laugh at yourself with your children. Let them see you are a human being too — not just a grown-up who rides tight herd on them.

As mothers we all make mistakes. We should be honest enough to admit them, and to apologize if necessary. Children are quick to forgive and even quicker to forget. This is a quality that most adults have lost along the way.

It's a good idea to have family councils where you can talk over grievances, problems and plans. The children can see that this is *their* family also and will bring about a sense of "togetherness" so rare in the world today. And we want our children to learn to *like* us as well as to *love* us. This closeness of purpose and heart can help bring this about.

THE MOTHER MUST ACCEPT EACH CHILD AS AN INDIVIDUAL. If God blesses our family with more than one child, we should accept the fact that they are different, separate beings. This is not an assembly line which we have to bathe, clothe and feed. Each child needs something different from us. He needs to feel that a part of us belongs to him and him alone. We can have many children and love them all the same amount with no partiality, yet our love for each child will be different, specially suited for that individual. We should try to give all of them some time of their own to be with us. And we should be able to keep their confidence on matters entrusted to us. Just because we are one family does not mean that we do not have private thoughts and even secrets which we do not share with others. Each child should feel secure in the knowledge that mother is here when she is needed. She knows his needs and what to do to help him or comfort him. He is loved; he is important to her; he is secure.

THE MOTHER SHOULD REMEMBER SHE IS ALSO A WIFE. Sometimes the tasks of motherhood become so pressing and continuous that we forget we are also wives. We should love our husbands and we should not be ashamed to let our children *know* we love him. We can help him be a better father because he is at a disadvantage in not being with them as much as we are. He does not have the chance to get to know them as intimately as we do. Both parents should share the responsibility of training the children; one must not be indulgent and the other strict. This can only bring disunity. We can even be guilty of pushing our husbands from our children's lives. We use him as a policeman, saying, "Just you wait till I tell your Daddy." They could become frightened of him to the extent that they never will become close to him.

If we have complaints about our husband's faults, we should never tell them to our children. He should not be criticized in front of them. Any differences between the parents should be settled privately and this is doubly important if the differences arise from the father's discipline of the children. Wait until he is through, then talk it over with him alone, never where the children might hear. Children sense discord very easily and react to it quite strongly. We should teach our children just how wonderful their daddy is and how hard he works for them because he loves them. Plan fun things which will include him. It might take a few private discussions before he learns the importance of appreciating the small things the children do but we should realize that he is busy all day coping with the really big job of making a living and it may be hard for him to come home and immediately adjust to the seemingly unimportant things the children do. This is where we can help him. It is our attitude toward our husband that will teach our children to respect him.

It's a great responsibility being a mother and a wife. We must accept all the tasks which face us in having children and training them and caring for them, but we must not forget that primarily, we are the companion of our mate. When our children are young, they take up a lot of our time but we must not shut our husband out of our lives. He must be made to feel that, while our time must be occupied with diapers, formulas and baby care, he is still the center of our heart. We will arrange a time when we can be together, for this is the core of our marriage.

It's a tremendous task, this job of motherhood. But we should never lose sight of the fact that women have been accomplishing big things since the beginning of time. History is full of the deeds and the influence of the female. And our own personal history can well read of the work we have done worthily in the eyes of man and God. Prayer is the greatest help we can have in being a mother. We cannot do what God would have us to unless we keep the line of communication open between us. We must read and study His word and then we must daily speak with Him for the wisdom, courage and strength to be the kind of mother which will make our children rise up and call us "Blessed."

SPECIAL ASSIGNMENTS

1.Have someone make a list of the opportunities available in your community for introducing your children to the finer things of life.

2. Have each member find some poem or quotation praising the mother. Put these in a small booklet and take to a home for the aged.

3. Have some member tell the story of a mother she has known who has proven herself worthy by God's standard.

STOP AND THINK

1. How does motherhood help woman become complete?

2. Why do you feel the mother has so much influence in the life of the child.

3. Taking II Timothy 1:5 as a guide, discuss the effect of a mother's teaching.

4. The law of nature says that physical ability to bear a child makes one a mother. How does God's teaching improve upon this basic concept?

5. Give your explanation of the Spanish proverb, "An ounce of the mother is worth a pound of the clergy."

6. Do you feel that Proverbs 22:6 is a positive promise? In the light of this, where do you think the responsibility for much of the juvenile delinquency be placed?

7. Why is example a better teacher than words?

8. Discuss some ways that the church might help the young women to be better mothers.

9. What do you think is the best kind of discipline? Why?

10. Since the woman is to be subject to her husband, he must be the first concern of her life. How can children fit into this relationship and still maintain the proper balance of husband first, all else second?

CHAPTER IV

THE IN-LAW

The road was dusty and hot as the three women walked along. There seemed to be a weight of despair surrounding them. Finally, the older of the three stopped and turning to the younger women began speaking earnestly with them. She was pleading with them to return to the homes of their mothers. The two younger women began weeping and shaking their heads. They were not willing to do this. After much discussion, one of them turned and walked slowly back the way the group had come, looking over her shoulder and weeping.

The older woman again turned to the younger and suggested that she follow the other back to their homeland. But this young woman had a determined manner about her. Though still weeping, she shook her head "No" putting her arms around the older woman, she looked deeply into her eyes and said, "Intreat me not to leave thee or to return from following after thee: for whither thou goest, I will go; and where thou lodgest, I will lodge: thy people shall be my people, and thy God my God. Where thou diest, will I die, and there will I be buried: the Lord do so to me, and more also, if ought but death part thee and me."

The women were Naomi and Ruth, mother and daughter-in-law and the tender speech was Ruth's vow given in Ruth 1:16-17. No lovelier piece of poetic literature has ever been written than the extraordinarily touching plea of this daughter-in-law. It has come down through the ages as a symbol of the two people joining their lives in unity and love for a common purpose. It is used in many marriage ceremonies today and we tend to forget that it was originally spoken by one woman to another. And these women were related in a way that would make the affectionate vow even more precious for they were in-laws!

The relationship of mother-in-law and daughter-in-law is a precarious one and seemingly, one that is burdened with a great many personality problems. Yet I believe that God included the story of Ruth and Naomi in His word, not only to give Ruth's part in the lineage of Christ, but to provide us with teaching on an association of life which has proven most difficult. Since Ruth and Naomi are the best examples we could possibly want, we will be using their lives as the pattern for our lesson on what God would have us be as an in-law.

THE DAUGHTER-IN-LAW. When a young girl marries the man of her choosing, she must leave father and mother and cleave unto him (Genesis 2:24). This is true of the young man also. Yet we cannot dismiss the parents of either as not being a part of the lives of the newly married couple. And while the two have become one, in a very real sense they have married all the family of each. For living involves not only the marriage relationship, but also the in-law affiliation. It is the wisdom with which this latter tie is handled that can mean either the complete happiness or dismal misery of the marriage.

Sad to say, but it is usually the mother-in-law and daughter-in-law relationship which gives the most difficulty. There are many psychological and sociological reasons for this but the basic cause probably lies in the fact that when a girl marries, her mother does not feel she is giving up her child, rather she is gaining another one. This does not seem to be true with the son and his mother. Almost without exception the boy's mother feels she is losing her child to another woman and thus, we find an almost ready-made situation for jealousy between the two women. The mother-daughter relationship changes very little after the young girl marries. But the mother-son tie undergoes quite a drastic change. Unless both the mother and the wife work at making their relationship a happy one, they will find themselves involved in a jealous triangle, with the poor young man caught between.

Being a good daughter-in-law is not an easy task. No woman likes to feel that she is being compared to another and yet it is only natural that the husband would see the difference between his bachelor life with his mother caring for him and his married life when his wife takes over the same job, but usually in a completely different manner. Here is where the husband must use wisdom in making the transition into this new life. But whether he does or not, the girl he has married must be willing to make the adjustments necessary to insure a peaceful, happy bond between his mother and herself.

And a strong bond it should be! After all, here is the woman who gave birth to the boy she loves. This mother cared for him, trained him, and guided his life so that he became the person she chose to give her life to. Since love is the greatest welding substance for any bond, the young wife should open her heart to the mother of her husband and be grateful for her part in making him what he is.

RUTH LOVED HER MOTHER-IN-LAW. We can see the great evidence of this affection by Ruth's decision to leave all she had known in order that she might accompany Naomi back to Bethlehem. Although Ruth was a Moabitess and thus a foreigner to her mother-in-law, she was able to overcome any differences this might have caused and truly came to love and respect Naomi. We are not told how long Ruth was married to Naomi's son, but we can see by her story that it was long enough for her to build a strong tie with his mother. This young girl was a pagan who had married into a God-fearing family, a situation which surely carried with it seeds of much discord. Yet her love for her mother-in-law was so great that she was willing to leave all the familiar things of her childhood and to accept Naomi's God as her God. Love served these two women well for it is the very basis of happiness in any union. With open heart, Ruth accepted Naomi and loved her. This made her voluntarily choose the life which was to cause her story to be recorded in divine history for our example. Love bound them together and enabled them to live together harmoniously.

RUTH SOUGHT HER MOTHER-IN-LAW'S COUNCIL. When Ruth chose to cast her lot with Naomi, she was willing to accept the responsibilities that went with it. When the two women reached Bethlehem, it was necessary for them to find a way to support themselves. Ruth was more able to work and was willing to do so. But she first came to Noami and sought her advice and permission in going out to glean for their sustenance. She could have felt that she was the one who had to do the work, so why ask Naomi about it. But this was not her attitude. She had given her life into the hands of her mother-in-law and she sought her counsel.

We should value the wisdom of older women who have matured in solving the problems of life. They have been along the road we are now traveling and can give us valuable assistance in guiding our lives in the right way. The daughter-in-law who seeks the counsel of her mother-in-law has made a wise decision, for God has admonished these older ones to guide the younger (Titus 2:3-5). She has shown herself to the mother-in-law as one who wants to do what is right and this will strengthen the bond of love between them.

RUTH WILLINGLY ACCEPTED THE COUNSEL OF HER MOTHER-IN-LAW. Because of her great love and respect for Naomi, Ruth trusted her in all that she did. When Naomi gave her instructions to seek Boaz' fulfillment of the law in taking his next of kin's inheritance, Ruth did not doubt that it was for her own good. She listened carefully and followed Naomi's advice. She could have been too proud to take this counsel on her love life. After all, this was private business and she could handle it herself. No, she knew that Naomi was wiser in this area than she. Therefore she was willing to do as she was instructed. And it was only in following Naomi's words that Ruth and Boaz were to find happiness. Boaz had made no effort to seek Ruth's hand in marriage. Only when Naomi told Ruth what she should do did Boaz feel that he could press his advantage as next of kin.

We know that all the advice given us by our mothers-in-law might not be right nor valuable. But we should have the attitude of heart to accept it as a gift of love. If she did not love her son, she would not be interested in the welfare of his family. She knows a great deal about him and can give wise counsel in helping with the difficulties of life and in adjusting to the marriage relationship. She lived *with* him and *for* him a long time before we came along. This gives her a valued insight into the things that we should know in order to make our life happy and acceptable to God.

RUTH INCLUDED HER MOTHER-IN-LAW IN HER LIFE. After Boaz had taken Ruth as his wife, Naomi was accepted as part of their family.

She was an integral part of their marriage and did much to assure their happiness. Ruth did not feel any jealousy of Naomi. She was included in the home life and played a very important role in raising the child of Ruth and Boaz. This child was to become the grandfather of David. By Naomi's love and care for Obed, she had a great influence on the future generations which came from the marriage of Ruth and Boaz. How foolish Ruth would have been to shut Naomi out of her life! She could have had her husband provide for her mother-in-law without taking her into their home. But Ruth's love for Naomi was brought to complete fullness when Naomi lived with them and cared for their child.

The wife today who will not include her mother-in-law in the life of her family is depriving them of one of God's blessings. We must allow our children to become the crown of the grandparents (Proverbs 17:6). If we shut out these wiser, older people, not only are we disobeying God's command to honor our parents and have respect for the elderly, but we have cut ourselves off from a source of love and wisdom. And in a world so bereft of these virtues, we cannot afford to do this.

RUTH HEEDED THE INFLUENCE OF HER MOTHER-IN-LAW'S LIFE. Naomi lived a life of goodness even in a pagan land. Her kindness was felt by the young girls who married her sons. They both came to love her very much. Even though Orpah turned back to her own family, she wept at the thought of leaving Naomi. What a wonderful influence this woman presented to the world! It made her a good wife and mother. It was her influence as a mother-in-law that made Ruth decide to cast her lot with God's people. Yet Ruth could have rejected this influence and returned to the idolatrous land where she was born. God-like principles can be exhibited before us by people who strive to be acceptable to His way and yet we can refuse to heed the example set. This would indicate a hardness of heart and a rebellious nature. Naomi's life represented all that was good to Ruth. She was wise enough to heed what she saw and it was this acceptance of the right influence that led Ruth to God's love and care.

THE MOTHER-IN LAW

The role of mother-in-law is perhaps the hardest which woman must fill in relationship to other people. This part in life has been the subject of much cruel and useless satire. So much so, in fact, that the term has become almost synonymous with unkind joking. As women, I suppose we will have to take the blame for this. The actions of too many mothers-in-law in the past have given much opportunity for such ridicule. It is a position in life which is hard to fill and one which draws very little sympathetic help. Yet Naomi was able to present herself in this role in such a way as to gain the crown of trust, honor and love. We shall look to her as our guide in being a good mother-in-law.

NAOMI ACCEPTED HER DAUGHTERS-IN-LAW FOR WHAT THEY WERE. Into the pagan land of Moab Naomi came with her husband and two sons. They had left Bethlehem because of the great famine in the land and now they were emigrants in an idolatrous land. All around Naomi were evidences of a life which she could not accept nor let her children embrace. As they grew older, they met and married two girls of this land. These girls were pagans, raised in idol worship and in a way foreign to the God of Naomi. Yet she must be a mother-in-law to these women. What a difficult task she faced! And only with great love for God was she able to undertake this and prove to her daughters-in-law that she was worthy of their love and respect.

How easily it would have been for Naomi to feel that she had nothing in common with Ruth and Orpah. After all, they were foreigners to her and as we are given to understand by the Bible, her sons had married them against the commands of God. God had forbidden the Israelites to marry outsiders but Mahlon and Chilion had chosen these girls because they were living in the land away from their own people. All this did not deter Naomi from being the kind of mother-in-law she should be. She accepted these two for what they were and went about her life in such a way as to make them love her. She knew that only when they came to love her would she ever be able to influence them for God.

She was able to accomplish this in the time before her sons died because we find in the beginning of the book of Ruth that both daughters-in-law felt great love for Naomi. When she decided to go back to Bethlehem, they were willing to go with her. In her willingness to accept Ruth and Orpah for their own selves and not for what she could make them become, Naomi was able to influence both of them for good. Though Ruth was the one who heeded the influence to make the decision to change her life, Orpah had a great respect and love for Naomi. She turned back to her own family, but it seems reasonable that the memory of this godly woman who had been her mother-in-law did much to sweeten her life. She did not make the change she should have, but the seeds of a godlike personality had been sown and perhaps they bore fruit in a way that we shall never know since the Bible does not record any further history of Orpah's life.

We will not be able to make the choice of a wife for our son. While we may see to it that he has the right kind of companions when he is growing up and that he is associated with Christian young people, the final decision for a mate will be his. She may not be the one we would have selected. Perhaps she is not even the right kind of girl. Yet if our son makes the choice and marries her against our counsel and advice, we must learn to accept her for what she is — hoping and praying that our influence might help change her. She is a human being in her own right and we must be able to look for the good that is certain to be there. The bad we will readily find, but we must search out the good and help bring it to the forefront in her life.

A mother-in-law once said the reason for all the friction she had with her son's wife came about because of her own theory of dealing with a young woman. She said, "I had always told myself that I would treat my in-laws just as I had my own children. I had thought this was a perfectly fair way to be and acted accordingly. After several years I found how mistaken I had been. For my in-laws were not my own children. They had not been raised as had mine; their training was not the same. Instead of accepting them as individuals, I began to treat them just as I had always treated my own, not realizing they were not used to that kind of relationship."

Every person is an individual and we must deal with each in the way that his nature dictates. With one we might be affectionate and friendly but with another, we must be more aloof. To try to force an alien attitude of personality on another is to almost certainly cause resentment. We may want to change our daughter-in-law but that change will only come after she learns to love and trust us for what we represent. Then will come the desire to emulate our life and thus the change can be made.

NAOMI LOVED HER DAUGHTERS-IN-LAW. Though the young women her sons chose to marry were not her choice, Naomi gave her heart in unselfish love. She did not harbor any jealousy toward those whom her sons had selected as mates. She loved them to the extent that she wanted only their good and when her sons died, she felt they could best be cared for by returning to their homes. And when Ruth chose to cast her lot with Naomi, this marked a new life for both of them. It was to be a life characterized by mutual love and concern for one another. Naomi loved Ruth and did all that she could to insure her future happiness. She arranged for Boaz to take the rights due him as next of kin. It was possible that this marriage would never have taken place had Naomi not taken the action she did. And this action came from a heart of love.

We, today, must accept the girl our son marries with real love and kind affection. Certainly she is deserving of this consideration since our child cares enough for her to select her as his life's companion. We might not be able to see all the qualities which endear her to him but if we do not withhold our genuine care and concern, then these qualities will become more evident to us as time passes. Perhaps we fail to see them bcause we are looking through a veil of jealousy. Shouldn't we look at this situation in another light? Our son is not taking us from his heart. He is merely asking us to move over just a little to make room for a more intimate relationship. This girl will not fill our place in his life. She has another role to fill and it is one which we cannot fulfill. Our place in his love remains the same; he has only increased his capacity to love others.

NAOMI SOUGHT ONLY GOOD FOR HER DAUGHTER-IN-LAW. Ruth was a Moabitess and as such was a foreigner in Bethlehem. She was an outsider and things could have been very bad for her had not Naomi been looking out for her good. Unselfish love gave Naomi every opportunity to seek that which was best for her daughter-in-law. She had allowed Ruth to accompany her back to her land because this was the only way Ruth would come under the care of God. In the wisdom of maturity, Naomi gave Ruth certain instructions in order that she might let Boaz know that he should accept his right as her next of kin. Her desire was not for herself but for her daughter-in-law. And this desire not only brought wonderful blessings to this daughter-in-law but in the last years of her life, it brought peace, contentment and great happiness to Naomi herself.

We should have this same attitude toward our daughter-in-law today. She has become a part of our family and we must do only that which can bring good to her. We must not be guilty of gossiping about her to others, whether the talk be founded or unfounded. She is one flesh with our son and we have no right to tear asunder what God has joined. We will act only with gentleness and kindness toward her. Our words will never be used against her but always for her benefit. To bring good to her is to bring the same to our son and this is what we desire. Our words and deeds must never prove otherwise.

NAOMI TRUSTED IN AND WAS TRUSTED BY HER DAUGHTER-IN-LAW. Perfect love can only be brought about if there is trust on both sides. Ruth knew she could trust her mother-in-law and for this reason she confided in Naomi. When Ruth had come in from the fields where she had been gleaning, she told all that was in her heart about how Boaz had treated her. Naomi was an interested and sympathetic listener. We have no indication that Ruth ever kept anything from Naomi and Naomi earned this trust by making certain she kept the confidences given her. When she knew that a way must be found to awaken Boaz to his responsibility toward Ruth, she devised a plan that showed just how great her trust was in her daughter-in-law. In asking Ruth to go and lay at Boaz' feet, Naomi was placing the young woman in a position that could have been immoral and open to danger. Yet Naomi did not fear because she knew both Ruth and Boaz were virtuous and the proper attitude would be maintained. What great trust she placed in Ruth!

The mother-in-law who stands aloof from the overtures made by her daughter-in-law should re-evaluate herself. We should keep ourselves ready for confidences and just as ready to assure that we can keep the confidence poured out to us. This relationship of loving trust between mother and daughter-in-law is one to be sought after and diligently worked for. Our attitude should be one of faithful assurance that we can be sought out for discussion of problems, seeking of counsel or merely confiding secret facts. The trust must be sincere and it must be mutual.

NAOMI MADE CERTAIN HER INFLUENCE WAS FOR GOOD. When woman was created, she was endowed with the ability to assert a great influence. She has been using that ability ever since. But influence can be either good or bad and it is up to the individual to choose which it will be and to work toward that objective. Influence is an active force, never passive. It is either right or wrong and not middle-of-the-road. We can be either an inducement for doing what is acceptable or the instrument which sanctions what is not acceptable. We are influencing someone every day of our lives. It may be for good or it may be for evil—but we are actively influencing all the time.

It was Naomi's influence which made Ruth decide to accept God and His ways. It was her good life which made this decision easier for her daughter-in-law. Through the principles which Naomi held dear, she brought about a happy marriage for Ruth and Boaz. There is no way to accurately estimate the power of a woman's influence. It is a fragile thing, to be carefully nurtured and protected. Yet it is a powerful force, moving people to great acts and wise decisions. It could be the element which might move our own daughter-in-law to accept the truth. Our words might fail to reach the heart, but our righteous life cannot help but touch a responsive chord in the lives of those dear to us.

NAOMI GAVE COUNSEL TO HER DAUGHTER-IN-LAW BUT SHE DID NOT BOSS HER. The relationship of Naomi and Ruth was one of mutual dependence. Ruth sought help and advice from her mother-in-law and Naomi was willing to give it. When Naomi saw the opportunity of giving counsel in a situation that could bring good to Ruth, she took advantage of this opportunity. She suggesed a method to Ruth of reaching Boaz, but she did not demand that Ruth take her advice. We see each of these women asking help of one another and giving this aid. Yet we cannot see any part of *bossing* or demanding in their attitudes.

As a mother-in-law we should stand ready to give help when called upon. And yes, there may be times when we can offer guidance or admonition even when not called upon to do so. (These "opportunities" must be carefully and prayerfully considered!) But in any case we should take the position of gentle advisor—desiring only the best for the loved one. And any advice or counsel should never be done in a belligerent, "do it *my* way" attitude.

In the story of Ruth and Naomi we can see how the love and mutual understanding of two women made for a contented, happy life. This is the story of a mother-in-law and a daughter-in-law. Should we not today be as zealous in making this relationship of life both pleasant and profitable? Not only will the geniality of this bond make for more wonderful earthly life, it could very well prove to be a factor in gaining eternal life for ourselves and the souls of our loved ones.

SPECIAL ASSIGNMENTS

1. Have someone make a report on what psychologists and socialists have to say about the role of the mother-in-law in our society today. The material for this can be found in the public library.

2. Have a panel discussion on the problems of the in-law, and how these might be solved through God's word.

3. Have two class members interview a Christian mother-in-law and a Christian daughter-in-law, seeking answers to what they feel are the qualities each should possess. Have these members give a report of her interview without disclosing who the interviewee is.

STOP AND THINK

1. Give at least two reasons why you think Ruth chose to go with Naomi.

2. In what way could the daughter-in-law's treatment of her husband's mother increase their own love for each other?

3. Do you think it is true that when you marry, you marry the whole family and not just a person? Discuss your reason.

4. Why do you feel that the mother-in-law and daughter-in-law relationship has more friction than the mother-in-law and son-in-law relationship?

5. Can a wife love her husband in a complete way without also loving his mother?

6. Why do you suppose so many daughters-in-law do not want any advice or counsel from their mothers-in-law?

7. Discuss several ways in which we could include our mother-in-law in our life.

8. In accepting a daughter-in-law for what she is, would this imply we must condone sinfulness on her part?

9. Although we cannot make the choice of a mate for our children, how can we influence their decision?

10. If we feel his choice is unwise, what can we do if he goes ahead and marries her?

CHAPTER V

THE TEACHER

The Bible class period was over. All the little children had passed from the room, going with their parents up to worship. Left in the room alone, the woman sat down on the small chair designed to fit her young pupils. Her mind went back over the past hour, searching for some feeling of achievement. Had the lesson been a success? Were the children interested? Did she ever have their full attention? These questions ran through her thoughts but she knew she could not tarry. Putting on her hat, she picked up her Bible and lesson book. Quietly she closed the door and walked up the steps to the main auditorium. Taking her place in a back pew, she saw one of her small pupils several rows ahead. The child was holding in his hand the "take-home" part of the lesson. The mother leaned over to the child and the teacher heard the little one say, "My teacher says God can help make me kind like the boy in this picture." "My teacher!" Such precious words to her ears. And yes, he had remembered what she had tried to impress upon him! Smiling, the teacher picked up the song book and prepared to begin her worship.

This scene, with some variations, is enacted in hundreds of church buildings every Lord's day morning. The feeling of having really *touched* the heart of her pupil is the highest award any teacher could have. The women teachers are so often the unsung heroes of our Bible class program. Taking the responsibility of sharing God's word with others is a blessing and privilege of which each woman in the church should avail herself. This is a role for which the woman is admirably suited and one that can bring the greatest amount of personal satisfaction in doing the work of the Lord.

It is the purpose of this chapter to inspire every Christian woman to prepare herself to be the best possible teacher. For in truth, each woman is a teacher in some capacity whether she recognizes the fact or not. For we actually are teaching something every time we come in contact with another person. Too long have we held the idea that to be a teacher we must stand before a class. Certainly, this is a most important phase of instructing in God's way, but it is not the only way. We may teach by the influence of our lives; we may teach privately to one or more people; or we may stand before a class. Each method is quite valuable and to win a soul to Christ often takes a combination of all of them.

WHO HAS THE RESPONSIBILITY OF TEACHING GOD'S WORD? This is the first question to be answered because too many of us tend to have the attitude of "Let George (or Mary or John or Susie) do it." If we hold to this idea, then it would be useless to delve into qualifications, methods and rewards. We must first realize that it is *our* responsibility and then we can go to these other matters.

In giving the great commission in Matt. 28:18-20, Jesus put the teaching on an individual basis. Each disciple was given the command to go and teach. They didn't go as a group and have one serve as the instructor. No, it was a personal matter. Paul, in writing to the Hebrew Christians, admonished them for still being pupils when they ought to be teachers (Hebrews 5:12). He was not chiding the preacher, the elders, or the deacons. He was speaking to each individual Christian. By reading this passage, we can see that there should come a time in each Christian's life when he must be a teacher.

God does not reach the souls of men in a miraculous way today. In establishing the church, He set in motion the machinery by which His word and His will should be taught. "To the intent that now unto the principalities and powers in heavenly places might be known *by the church* the manifold wisdom of God" (Ephesians 3:10). The church is the instrument through which man might learn what God wants of him. Since the church is made up of living stones (the individual), then we can see the responsibility to teach others is enjoined upon every person who has been baptized into Christ and thus added to His church. This means both male and female — each Christian must teach. His responsibility would be proportionate to his God-given abilities or talents, but even the one talent person must use that.

WHAT LIMITATIONS ARE PLACED ON WOMEN TEACHERS? Since we recognize the fact that women must be teachers, we must then verify the circumstances under which she may instruct. Does God limit her activity in this sphere? If so, what are these limitations? The Bible can give us many examples of women who taught God's way and from these we find that He does expect us to fill a place in His work. In the Old Testament we see Miriam who led the women in praise of God. It seemed to be her special duty to instruct them in what God wanted. During the period of the judges, God allowed Deborah to serve in the capacity of prophetess-judge. And later under king Josiah, God spoke to the people through Huldah, another prophetess and teacher.

We do not have to limit our examples to the Old Testament, however for we have many in the New. The first woman teacher mentioned in the New Testament is Anna. She was the prophetess who was in the temple at the time Mary and Joseph brought baby Jesus in for the rite of purification. She recognized Jesus as the Redeemer and from that time it is said she spoke of him to all who were looking for the Messiah. She had found the promised one and spent her life teaching others about him.

Perhaps the woman teacher we are most familiar with is Priscilla. In Acts 18:24-26 the story is told how the eloquent Jew, Apollos, was taken aside and taught the way of truth more perfectly by Priscilla and her husband, Aquila. Here was a woman who, with her husband, was full of strength and courage when it came to serving God. They were not afraid to approach Apollos and teach him. We have every reason to believe that Priscilla had an important part in this instruction, for why else would God allow her name to be recorded in His word?

In the 21st chapter of Acts we are told about Philip's four daughters who were teachers, or who prophesied. These four girls were raised in a godly home for their father was one of the seven men chosen to help the apostles in the menial work of the church in Jerusalem. They had learned of Christ and were ready to share the responsibility of telling others. Not only are we given examples of women who taught, but we also have the positive command from God to teach. Titus 2:3-6 gives the older women the instruction to teach the younger.

God does have a place for the woman teacher, but He also places certain limitations upon her. She may teach in any capacity which does not violate this order of authority. "Let a woman learn in silence with all submissiveness. I permit no woman to teach or have authority over men; she is to keep silent. For Adam was formed first, then Eve, and Adam was not deceived, but the woman was deceived and became a transgressor. Yet woman will be saved through bearing children, if she continues in faith and love and holiness, with modesty" (I Timothy 2:11-12). The woman cannot teach the man nor act in any way that would cause her to have the authority over him.

Does this mean we cannot teach a man privately? It would not seem so, for did not God give us the example of Priscilla who helped teach Apollos privately? And there may came a time when a woman is the only person available to teach some man. We should be ready for this opportunity but we must not teach a class of men, taking their rightful leadership. God's position for women from the beginning lets us know that we are to be subject to man and not allowed to usurp his authority.

There are several ways that woman can take the authority from man as a teacher. We might teach without the approval or consent of the elders. We can refuse to recognize the husband as the head of the family. We can allow ourselves to be rebellious to man and not follow the rules and suggestions made for our good. Or we might dominate man by acting in such a way as to show that we do not respect the relative positions of the man and woman. Any of these situations would find us teaching in direct disobedience to God's will for us.

As a woman I have a definite place in teaching others about God, Christ and the church. I must not shirk my duty but I must not go beyond the bounds which God has placed for my own good. These are the basic rules which govern me when I serve as an instructor in God's service. But there are other qualifications which the teacher should meet, as well as some pitfalls we want to avoid. Let us look at some of these requirements.

THE TEACHER MUST HAVE PERSONAL FAITHFULNESS. Before we can teach in any capacity, we must make certain that our lives meet God's standard of acceptance. How can we teach faithfulness and a love of God to others if we show by our way of living that He is only second best. John Ruskin stated, "Teaching is a continual and difficult work to be done by kindness, by watching, by warning, by precept, and by praise, but above all — by example." People will accept more readily what we teach by word if our living backs it up with the proper example. The poet Edgar Guest put it aptly when he wrote, "I'd rather see a sermon than hear one any day." To teach others we must first have guided our own way of life into an acceptable pattern. Then we like Paul could say, "Be ye followers of me, even as I also am of Christ" (I Corinthians 11:1).

THE TEACHER MUST HAVE A LOVE FOR SOUL-SAVING. This is a most vital prerequisite to teaching. We must love the souls of people before we will ever be effective in reaching them for Christ. This is not always easy to do because as human beings, we tend to look at the personality of the person rather than looking inward to the soul. The personality is only temporary; it will return to the dust. But the soul is eternal and will live forever — either in the presence of God or in torment away from God. The desire to save the souls of the people we meet should be uppermost in our hearts and minds. We should be willing to make any sacrifice necessary or adjust our life in any way that would enable us to reach that precious soul. Paul loved the Jewish nation so much that it was his heart's desire and prayer that they might be saved (Romans 10:1). It was this great emotion that made him endure all things that others might obtain the salvation which is in Christ (II Timothy 2:10). Until we have this love for the souls of others, we will never become the potent force for God that He desires.

THE TEACHER MUST HAVE A KNOWLEDGE OF THE BIBLE AND A RESPECT FOR ITS POWER. It is almost unnecessary to state that we cannot teach a person something we ourselves do not know. Yet by the actions of many Christians, we might feel it is needful to remind us of this adage. We do not study the Bible as we ought so the lessons we teach are only shallow bits of the knowledge contained therein. We could not delve into the depths of its wisdom for our students because we have never learned to "swim" there ourselves. Too many of us are satisfied with skimming our way through God's word, never tasting of the riches it contains. Study is the only way to reach the depths of God's wisdom as it is held in His word. And study is hard work and takes self-discipline. Moreover, it is the way which God tells us that we may show ourselves approved unto Him (II Timothy 2:15). Perhaps we fail to accept this fact as a positive command but in so doing, we will gain the disapproval of our heavenly Father. We cannot know how to use His word if we do not study. There is nothing more positive than this.

The more we study the Bible, the more powerful it becomes to us. We can see the great force lying within its pages, waiting to be released by someone willing to use it. The word of God is the most powerful thing known to man. It can touch the life of a human and change it from all the ugliness of sin to the beauty of a pure, forgiven being. It can motivate man to the highest deeds because it works in love. The Bible contains God's will for us and as such, is the greatest, most potent force in the world. Why? Because it is the power of God unto salvation (Romans 1:16). Only within His word can we find what we must do to be saved. And because of this, it should be the most valuable of any possession. More important, it should be written in the heart and mind so that we may have the force available to give to others.

THE TEACHER MUST UNDERSTAND THE NEEDS OF THE STUDENTS. The art of being eloquent does not mean the person will be a good teacher. True, we must be able to communicate God's word by both action and word, but we must know something beyond the words we speak. The most effective teacher is the one who senses the needs of the student and thus gears the lesson accordingly. This is why women are so ably suited to teach the young children, the teenage girl, and the women's classes. We understand the requirements and desires of these groups and can more readily fit the lesson to the need. Paul knew when to feed his listeners milk and when they were ready for meat. He did not force the "meat" of the word on the young Christian. It was not suited to him and would therefore do him no good. As teachers we must try to develop that sixth sense which gives us an insight into the thinking of those we are trying to teach. We can learn more of this by getting to know the student also. If we do not have this understanding, we will not be very effective. Developing it will take some time and personal interest in the individual. But it will prove worthwhile if we can help solve the problems of even one person.

Not only must we learn to fit the lesson to the need of the student, but when we present it we must see that our attitude is one that will make the lesson acceptable to them. Every teacher should memorize the passage of scripture found in II Timothy 2:24-25. It should be the motto of anyone teaching another. "And the servant of the Lord must not strive; but be gentle unto all men, apt to teach, patient, in meekness instructing those that oppose themselves; if God peradventure will give them repentance to the acknowledging of the truth." Gentleness and patience — two elements of vital importance in bringing the truth to others. Putting all the elements of successful teaching together, we should stand ready to "spend and be spent" for the saving of souls (II Corinthians 12:15).

THE FOUR P'S OF SUCCESSFUL TEACHING. One able teacher gave a formula which she used in her teaching program. It was so concise and worthwhile, I am passing it on to you.

A. Preparation — II Timothy 2:15
B. Prayer — I Peter 3:12
C. Patience — II Timothy 2:24
D. Perseverance — Galatians 6:9

Not only are there many positive things we must do before becoming a good teacher, but there are also a number of things which we should avoid. These are things which can be learned by experience but would save each of us a lot of time and concern if we would learn from what others have discovered in their work.

THE TEACHER MUST NOT TEACH TO PROJECT HERSELF. Although there is a great deal of personal satisfaction to be gained from teaching we must guard against using this work as a "showcase" for our abilities. What we are teaching is more important than any praise we might get for being an eloquent speaker or presenting a lesson in a dramatic manner. We are not trying to project our own egos to the class, but rather the picture of the glory of God and His love for man. If we present a lesson to display ourselves, we are misusing the talents which God has given us. The teacher is never as important as what she is teaching.

This brings to mind the fact that as women we are very interested in clothing and appearance. We like to be well-dressed and spend a great deal of time on making ourselves attractive. All this is well and good — if we do not detract from the lesson. Our clothing should not be such as to bring the student's attention away from what we are saying. This is especially true if we wear a hat while teaching a class. It is usually better to teach bareheaded and then put the hat on before going in to worship, especially if you are teaching the younger children. With teenagers and women, this is not necessary if the hat is of such design so as not to distract the class. If the student remembers more about our clothing than about the lesson, we have failed to teach that day — and we cannot afford to lose that time!

THE TEACHER SHOULD NOT EXPECT TOO MUCH NOR TOO LITTLE OF HER STUDENTS. It is not always true that the teacher is the best informed person in the class. Certainly she will have the lesson well prepared through periods of study and when she faces her class, she is ready to present this to the pupils. Her attitude should be one of expecting the best from her class. If they are new Christians or younger children, she must not expect them to have a knowledge of "meat" nor even a thorough understanding of the "milk." The teacher should have the right to expect her students to have prepared their lesson in advance, but she should not presume they have higher understanding than their growth level would indicate. We have to realize that if our students are children, they have other activities and the lessons we ask them to study should be geared accordingly. If they are women, we know their time is also limited and the same would apply to them.

There is a balance which should be maintained in what we can expect from the student, but I feel that most of the time we do not expect enough. Too many of us are not really making the effort necessary to prepare ourselves for any kind of Bible study and then we are ashamed when we cannot answer a question put to us by the teacher. This should spur us on to learning more — leaving the milk diet behind and preparing for the meat diet. As a teacher, we do not want to embarrass anyone by asking something we feel they cannot answer. We should try to phrase the question in such a way as to guarantee that the student can give some kind of an answer and then we can build on that answer.

THE TEACHER SHOULD AVOID AN UNWISE CHOICE OF MATERIALS. This goes back to fitting the need to the lesson. To teach a course on Christian motherhood to a class of little girls would provide a very poor learning situation. The students are not ready for this material and the decision to use it would be unwise. If the class is either physically or mentally unprepared for what we are using, we should look elsewhere for better material. Another great fault of this nature is in presenting lessons which are not mature enough for the class. This is especially true in teaching the teenage group. We should give them practical lessons in putting Christianity into action. Most of them have had Bible stories and learned Bible facts in their earlier years in Bible classes. Now they need to know how to translate these stories and facts into useful observations and lessons on living their life. If we cannot find any material we think is suitable, we should have the courage to prepare a series on our own. More Christian teachers are doing this and we now have a wider selection of materials to choose from. Yet if we know what we want to say to our particular class and can find nothing conforming to our desires, we should stand ready to prepare it, submit it to the elders for approval and then teach it to the class.

THE TEACHER SHOULD NOT BECOME DISCOURAGED. In the discussions held at teachers' meetings, there will almost always be a good teacher who says, "I think I will give up my class. I'm so discouraged. They don't listen to me: I'm not getting anywhere." How often I've felt this way myself! The object of being a teacher after all is making certain the pupil learns. If we feel that this is not taking place, we are depressed and ready to give up. We must not give in to this feeling of despair. I firmly believe it is the tool of the devil — discouragement. Let us recognize it as such and lift ourselves above it. No one has ever had any more reason for despair than the great apostle Paul, yet he said, "We are troubled on every side, yet not distressed; we are perplexed, but not in despair . . . " (II Corinthians 4:8).

When we feel that something is wrong and we are not accomplishing what we should, then we should lift our hearts in prayer for strength and courage and perhaps more insight. Yes, insight to evaluate our teaching and see if the fault lies there. Maybe we have not met the needs of our students.

Perhaps the material is not correct for them. Our attitude or our method of presentation might be wrong. But these are things we can correct, and correct them we must if we see they exist. Discouragement has no place in the life of the teacher. It wastes too much time and time is too valuable to us. Let us put behind us those things which bring us depression and correct those that are necessary and then press on to the goal which we have before us.

THE REWARD FOR TEACHING FAR OUTWEIGHS THE EFFORT. The blessings which God promised us for obedience to His commands are always greater than the trials and troubles we might have to go through to make ourselves acceptable. Though the condemnation for teaching wrongly will be greater (James 3:1), the rewards for leading others to God are rich indeed. Perhaps the greatest earthly joy we could know would be in winning a soul to Christ. There are no words to describe the feeling the heart possesses when you witness the baptism of someone you have taught. You have given the greatest gift possible to this one and yet you have a blessing which cannot be valued.

When we use the ability to teach, God will increase that talent. (Matthew 25:29). We may start out shaky, frightened and weak in words, but to start is the most important part. Using any ability will improve and enrich it. Each opportunity we take of teaching others will make us more ready to accept the next challenge which comes our way.

The most important personal reason for teaching is the preservation of our souls. God tells us that if we do not bear fruit, we will be cut off and burned. The souls of others are the fruit we present to God from a life of service. And teaching is the farming that brings forth that necessary fruit.

There are many ways in which we can teach God's word. We can teach by the influence of our life. This is necessary and good but it alone will not tell another what he must do to be saved. Our teaching must also be by positive words. These can be spoken before a class or to a small group in the home. They may be said to one of our children or to our friends and neighbors. There is practically no limitation to where they might be uttered. The thing to remember is that they *must* be said. We will surely make mistakes; most everyone does. Yet the mistakes come from doing the work. The greatest sin is doing nothing.

An unknown poet wrote these words and I would like to close this lesson by sharing them with you:

> A builder builded a temple; He wrought with care and skill;
> Pillars and groins and arches were fashioned to meet his will;
> And men said when they saw its beauty: "It shall never know decay.
> Great is thy skill, O Builder, thy fame shall endure for aye."

A teacher builded a temple; she wrought with skill and care;
Forming each pillar with patience, laying each stone with prayer.
None saw the unceasing effort; none knew of the marvelous plan;
For the temple the teacher builded was unseen by the eyes of man.

Gone is the builder's temple: crumbled into dust,
Pillar and groin and arches food for consuming rust;
But the temple the teacher builded shall endure while the ages roll;
For that beautiful, unseen temple was a person's immortal soul.

SPECIAL ASSIGNMENTS

1. Have each member bring a poem or quotation on Teacher or Teaching and put these in a small scrap book. Present this to a godly woman who has given many years to teaching the Bible.

2. Have a report given on some of the materials available for the use of the Bible class teacher. Many of the book stores and publishing firms have catalogs. Perhaps if there is not a book store in your town, your minister or educational director could give this report.

3. Give one whole class period to study of woman's part in doing personal work. Special assignments might be given to several on: How women can do personal work, Why we should do personal work, Ways of doing personal work.

STOP AND THINK

1. Why is the individual so important in teaching God's plan of redemption?

2. Do you feel that women should be allowed to teach young boys? teenage boys?

3. Would there be any value in a person "specializing" by teaching a certain age level or some particular Bible lesson series? Why?

4. List some personal qualifications for teachers of the following groups: Nursery, Teenage, Women.

5. If the Great Commission applies to the individual, how can women fulfill it without usurping man's authority?

6. Would teaching a man in a cottage class be usurping this authority? Why?

7. Why is example such a worthy teacher?

8. How is the most powerful force known to man made available to him?

9. Do you feel that every person should be able to teach a class in the Bible class program? Discuss.

10. What special opportunities are available in teaching for the woman? How is she better suited for some of these than man?

CHAPTER VI

THE WORKER IN THE CHURCH

The sound of the mourners filled the house. In the upper room lay the body of a woman beloved by all of them. Her death had brought her friends together and the group sadly discussed the wonderful qualities of their loved one. A man walked into the room and the whisper spread, "Here is Peter!" Immediately all the widows began to show Peter the clothing which the dead woman had made, crying all the while. He asked to be alone with their friend and as they left, they saw him kneeling beside her bed. Outside the door the women clustered together, waiting and wondering. The door opened and Peter's voice called to them. When they entered the room, there was Dorcas, alive and well. The word rapidly spread throughout the city of Joppa and "many believed in the Lord" (Acts 9:36-42).

God has allowed this portrait of the noble woman, Dorcas, to be preserved for our learning. We should be so grateful, for in giving us this picture of Dorcas, He has shown woman at work in the church. And no grander portrayal of this role of womankind could ever be given. In looking about for some service to perform in the work of the Lord, we too often overlook the "little" things depicted in the story of this good woman. But nothing is "little" in the eyes of God and He has recorded the work of Dorcas to help us learn this lesson.

DO WOMEN HAVE A PLACE IN THE WORK OF THE CHURCH? This seems like a needless question to put forth yet we only have to look at the idleness of a great many Christian women to see that perhaps it has not been answered in their minds. In looking at the early church we ascertain that God had a place and purpose for everyone. Those set in the church first were assigned their tasks. The apostles gave their time in prayer and the ministry of the word (Acts 6:4). II Timothy 4:3-5 gives the responsibilities of the evangelists and the elders and deacons are delegated to serve in certain areas also (Acts 20:28 and Acts 6:1-2). Yet God did not leave out the individual members of the church. We have studied in previous lessons the obligations of the individual. Read I Corinthians 12:12-30 and you will find the Lord impressing each Christian with finding his own place and filling it without jealousy. And since women were included in those who first obeyed Christ, then we can only conclude that we have a place to fill, a work to do. Whether we be the "eye" or the "hand" or even a "toe" we will function in that spot diligently and tirelessly. We must not let down the other members of His body.

There are many examples of women in the New Testament church doing varied but important jobs. Dorcas, who made clothing for the needy, has already been mentioned. We see Lydia, the successful business woman, who helped start a new congregation in Philippi. Phoebe is commended as a deaconess, or servant, of the church at Cenchrea. We do not know what specific work she did, but we can be sure she was occupied with something worthwhile if Paul felt he could call her a servant of the Lord. Paul also mentioned two women, Euodia and Syntyche, who labored with him in Philippi. And then we know of Lois and Eunice, homemakers, who so ably trained young Timothy. These women bear testimony to the diversity of the tasks which we can undertake for God.

WOMAN'S WORK IN THE CHURCH IS AN INDIVIDUAL RESPONSIBILITY. The vivid portrayal of the church as a body in I Corinthians 12 demonstrates the individual responsibility of the Christian in serving God through the work of the church. By this we see that *every* person has some ability to serve and unless that ability is exercised and allowed to grow and mature, it will be taken away. The parable of the talents helps us understand that our responsibility is in direct proportion to our ability. God expects of me only that which I can fulfill. He does not set a standard of abilities and then require each to live up to it. In His wisdom He gives everyone certain talents and that person has the obligation to use that with which he was endowed. The parable does teach, however, that any talent used will be multiplied or increased while the unused ability will be taken away.

Not only must each woman fill her own place with what God has blessed her, but she has to make certain that her work is done under the oversight of the elders. She is an integral part of the body of Christ and has opportunities and obligations which she must accept but these must be discharged within the framework of God's order of authority. She cannot usurp the rightful dominion of man by any task in which she engages. This would mean she must not take away the power of the elders in doing any work. God is the head of all; Christ is the head of the church and man is the head of the woman. This is the order which has been divinely ordained for our own good and any work we do must fit within this harmonious arrangement.

WOMAN'S FIRST WORK IS FOUND IN MAKING A CHRISTIAN HOME. A careful study of the New Testament reveals that woman's best place of service is in her home. This is the sphere for which she was created and for which she is suited. Before any woman can begin to found a godly home, she must look to her own character. Proverbs 31 is a valuable source for the characteristics which we must possess as Christian women. We will summarize these briefly here: The woman of God must be chaste, pure and virtuous in her life. She will love God and accept Him as an active force in her home. She will be discreet, able to be trusted — certainly not a gossip. People will trust her because she can keep confidences. This woman will be kind and gentle; her compassion will lead her to help others. In the New

Testament we find more personal qualities of such a woman. She is described as a light in the world and a leavening influence among all she meets. She will be moderate in her actions and concerned with the welfare of others. If she incorporates these things into her life, she will have an excellent foundation on which to build her home and the writer of the Proverbs says that if we are wise, we will *build* our house, not tear it down. If these virtues are found in us, then we might truly "walk within our house with a perfect heart" (Psalms 101:2).

The home is the arena of life in which woman most adequately displays the talents which God has given her. To provide a clean, happy place of abode for a loved husband and precious children is the noblest of all the tasks which we might accept. To be a thrifty and industrious housekeeper is as much a work of the Lord as teaching a class or visiting the sick. The hospitality which is shown in a Christian home can do much to win the confidence of people who can then be taught the positive commands of the gospel. The Christian homemaker uses each opportunity to entertain with meals, showers or teas as a direct service to God. Her home life might also enable her to fulfill other commands of God by taking care of parents or needy children or widows. All this fits into the pattern of work God has outlined for us in making us "keepers at home."

It is in the home that the mother does her most effective teaching. Daily she will find the time to impress upon her children the loving kindness of God. She will help them by her training to understand the truths necessary for their salvation. In her own little castle she will move in such a way as to be the saving influence of an unbelieving husband. Her friends and neighbors will learn about Christ over a friendly cup of coffee. The milkman, the postman, the cleaning man — all can come closer to a knowledge of God by observing the life of the Christian wife and mother. How then can we say that woman is not serving God by making a good home?

We must add a word of admonition here. God has blessed us with this home; He has seen fit to give us these children to love and train. We know that we must use our time wisely and well in doing His work and this work includes being a good wife and mother. But we should be cautious lest we begin to use these obligatory blessings as an *excuse* for not serving God in other ways! In the early years of our children, it is necessary for more time to be given to their care. But even in these years, there are other tasks we should accept, other jobs which we can perform. As the children grow older, more of our time can be free for these works. To shut ourselves in our homes and live for only what is found within its walls would be closing our eyes and hearts to the numerous activities which we can — and must — fit into our lives in order to more perfectly serve God.

TEACHING IS AN IMPORTANT WORK WOMAN MAY DO. The previous chapter dealt with teaching as a work responsibility of the Christian woman. For this reason we will not spend a great deal of space on this particular area of service. We would reiterate that women are more ably suited to teach the small children, teenage girls and other women. She can do this in either a public or private way as long as she does not step outside the pattern of authority laid down by God. This sphere of ministry not only enriches the life and mind of the student but it develops the teacher's heart, mind and abilities. You cannot teach others without learning much for yourself. We can learn how to teach by employing several aids. It is useful to sit in on actual class periods as a helper, observing a good teacher at work. There are usually teacher training workshops available several times a year in the larger cities. Magazines containing helps from experienced instructors are published each month. Many congregations provide these for their teachers and those interested in learning how to teach. After we acquire a knowledge of the principles of superior teaching, it is time to make the "plunge" and start teaching. Experience is always the best teacher and coupled with fervent prayer, we can exercise our abilities into more acceptable godliness.

Personal work is an important task which women can adequately perform. We should learn enough to be able to tell another what they must do to be saved. If we feel we do not have the ability to speak in our own words, there are film strip series which we can use. But women can serve in an important capacity in this work. We can have cottage meetings in our homes for a neighborhood group. Or if we just feel we cannot do this, we can always set up such a class and find someone else to teach it. This work must be done and women have opportunities to do it that men never have. We meet people our husbands will never have the chance to teach. If we fail to let these people know of Christ, they may never come in contact with the church again. Special opportunities are ours in reaching others with the gospel. Let us seek these out, recognize them when they come our way and do our best to assume the responsibility.

WOMEN PLAY AN IMPORTANT PART IN THE BENEVOLENT WORK OF THE CHURCH. The benevolent work of the church is especially suited to womankind. She is endowed with the qualities which make her fitted to serve others. Her gentle touch in caring for the older people, her loving manner in helping the orphans, her kind words in comforting the sorrowing — all these are the distinctive characteristics which make her superior in this particular area of Christian endeavor.

We can take the material articles necessary for a family in need and present these to them in a kind, loving manner. Women can be more at ease in this situation than men. When the elders set this need to be fulfilled, the women should stand ready to be the willing emissaries to those who are destitute. We can sew the garments for people like Dorcas did before us. We can cook meals for those who are ill. We can mail out cards to those in sorrow or who might be sick. We can provide transportation to those who do not have their own.

The seemingly small but necessary tasks which must be done can be passed to the women because they have more time to give. We could not begin to mention all the benevolent work which can be done. If we really want to serve though, we can let this fact be known to the elders, the minister, or someone who has charge of this work. We can be assured that there will be something for us to do!

HOSPITALITY IS A WORTHY WORK. "Use hospitality one to another without grudging" (I Peter 4:9). This is an area where we really come into our prime, for women love to "pretty up" their homes and fix special dishes for company. And God has commanded us to be hospitable. He even says "some have entertained angels unawares" by showing cordiality to strangers. Our homes should be used to the glory of God, whether we have a decorator furnished house or apple crate furniture. Our husbands cannot be gracious if we do not stand ready to back them up. The largest part of this falls upon the wife. But this is a blessing which we can give our husbands and we will be serving them, our guests and God.

Our homes should be open for meals to newcomers, old friends, visiting preachers and even strangers. The hospitality extended should not be done on a "now you owe me a dinner" basis. Rather as Christ suggested, we should have those who have no possibility of repaying our cordiality to them. If we get a return invitation, we have already received the blessing from our own hospitality.

We should allow our children to be hosts in their own home. If we have older children, we can provide good recreation for them by having parties, dinners and get-togethers for their own age groups. We can assist the teachers of our smaller children by opening our homes to their social needs. Hospitality can be shown in many ways — both by deeds and attitudes. It is up to us to seek out the best ways we can use it.

VISITATION IS AN IMPORTANT WORK FOR WOMEN. The most active visitation programs of most congregations are carried out by the women. They have more time and an easier manner in doing this work and only eternity will reveal the value of work done by these good people. A personal visit is one of the most beneficial ways of reaching people for Christ. A telephone call is good and serves its purpose, but a person-to-person conversation has a quality which is hard to equal. There are the newcomers we can call on. If they have visited the congregation, it will make them feel noticed if we come to their home shortly after they worship with us. Our friendly attitude tells them, "We were so happy to get to know you. Won't you let us get better acquainted with you?"

There are others who need our personal attention. The weak member needs the strength which we can give them by being concerned with their absence. Perhaps they have problems which we might help solve and this in turn might help them mature and become faithful. There are those who are ill who would enjoy a short visit from us. We might even take a small gift — a scrapbook we have made of inspirational poems or some hand-made article or home-cooked delicacy. This is true with the shut-in also. Since these people come in contact with the outside world only through their visitors, we should make certain our visits are cheerful, positive experiences. And we must also call upon those who are bereaved. This is a difficult time and they need all the help we can offer. If we cannot find the words to comfort them, we can let them know we love them and are concerned with their heartache. We should remember these later, also, after time has passed. We can give them booklets on sorrow which will help them face this time. We do not want them to feel we have forgotten them after the immediate tragedy is over. Old people, shut-ins, visitors, strangers in town, all these provide excellent opportunities for personal visits which can strengthen the caller as well as the called upon.

WOMEN ARE ABLY SUITED TO COUNSEL OTHERS. The tender compassionate nature of woman makes her an excellent counselor. She has the understanding of the problems which face her sex and should prepare herself to guide others along a way she has come. It is the duty of all Christians to help restore someone who has fallen. "Brethren, if a man be overtaken in a fault, ye which are spiritual, restore such an one in the spirit of meekness; considering thyself, lest thou also be tempted" (Galatians 6:1). The process of bringing such an individual back to the service of God would include counseling. We can serve in this capacity to young girls with their special problems. Our manner should be one of confidence in God, not in our own wisdom. Counseling from our own thoughts would be like the "blind leading the blind" and we should make certain that we seek God's wisdom in guiding others. The older women must give the necessary counsel to the younger. From the wealth of experience of life and knowledge of God, the mature can function worthily in helping others with advice and guidance.

LOOK AROUND FOR THE "SMALL" THINGS. It has been said that it is the "small" things which back up and surround the big things, and without them, the important things could not operate. This can well be applied to the work of the church. There are numerous detail jobs which cry out for help to get them done. The weekly bulletin can use the helping hands of the woman. She can gather the material for it, type the stencil and run it on the mimeograph machine. This same service can be performed for some of the teachers who need lessons duplicated. These same teachers could probably use some help in cutting out their weekly lesson materials, or pictures from magazines to make their stories more vivid to the children.

The church office is full of little chores with which the women can help. We can do typing for the preacher; we can make visitation schedules and files. There are envelopes to be stuffed with mailing to the membership, stamps to be stuck on. Perhaps there are lesson or song books which need mending. Another worthy task is the care of the baptismal clothing, making certain it is clean and available at all times. Most congregations have a nursery provided for the young children. This is full of jobs which we can do. There are the necessary supplies we can bring and the linens to be kept fresh and clean. New toys can be supplied or the old ones cleaned and mended. Look around, or better still, ask around. The work is there and you will not only be serving God but receiving a blessing for yourself in accepting the responsibility for anything that needs to be done.

EACH WOMAN MUST FIND AND FILL HER PLACE. Since there are jobs for every woman who will take the responsibility, it is necessary for each of us to seek out that which we can do. First, we can take a look at our talents in a completely honest manner. What am I best suited to do? Where do my interests lie? Can I learn to do a particular work? We will naturally do best those things for which we are equipped and these should be the tasks we pursue first of all. Yet we should recognize the fact that we may have hidden abilities and be on the lookout for opportunities to enrich our service by tackling new work. If we find a situation for which we are totally unprepared and unfitted, then we will keep looking and trying. Perhaps several "trial and error" circumstances will be our experiences before we find that for which we are seeking. But we should never be afraid or ashamed to accept a new challenge. It might just be that this would be exactly your place to serve. We can find new areas of service by attending training classes, by observing the work of women in other congregations and by going to one of the lectureships held each year by the Christian colleges. If we see something we feel interested in, search out an experienced person and ask if you might work with them for a while. But in exploring new fields of service, we should never feel too proud to accept "little" jobs. These need to be completed also and who knows, perhaps from preparing ourselves for these "little" jobs, we will come face to face with the "big" one we can do. The great man Albert Schweitzer once said that no man has the right to accept large tasks if he cannot apply himself diligently and patiently to the small ones.

THERE ARE NEGATIVE AREAS OF WOMEN'S WORK. As in any activity, we must avoid certain things which will keep us from performing at our peak level. This is most true with our work in the church. In any thing we accept to do, we must be careful not to make a great show of ourselves. This is not the purpose of the Christian life. The motive in any function of the work of the Lord should be a great love of Christ and the souls of men and not for any selfish reason. There is no place for the ego-maniac in this employment. God first, others second, me third. This should be the creed of our Christian calling. It is our resolve to present Christ to the world and not project our own personality. This should be lost in the beauty of the love we offer a lost and dying world.

A self-righteous attitude will hinder any work undertaken for the Lord. This was not Christ's position and if we want to be like Him, it cannot be ours. The woman who is working in the church to build her own ego is misplacing her love and loyalty. A spirit of humility, gentleness and love will be the most effective in searching out and teaching those who need our Saviour. Our "See what I'm doing" attitude will not only cause us to lose the blessings we might ourselves receive from our work, but it will most surely cause discouragement, discontent and even dislike in others working with us. We must lose ourselves in the depths of His teachings. Then, and only then, will our service be acceptable and successful in His sight.

Whatever task we accept, we should do it with all our might. Zeal should be the common characteristic of every woman serving the Lord. Our work should not be done grudgingly but it should be a way of life. This is the secret of the Christian and it is the key to acceptance by God. Impatience or dissatisfaction with any thing assigned to us marks us as trying to put selfish desires above the needs of the church. Maybe our choice is not as noticeable to others and thus, we get no praise. Should this deter us? Must we be immature and demand commendation for any little thing we do? God's word teaches that if we receive the praise and glory of man, this is our reward for our service. It will be the things unsung and unnoticed by man which will lay up treasures in heaven for us. Wholeheartedly we should be able to sing, "We will do with our might what our hands find to do." The need is ever-present; each day will present new opportunities. Let us each find our place and after finding it, fill it with all the ability which God has given us.

SPECIAL ASSIGNMENT

1. Have two of the women search out and make a list of the work which the women in your congregation can do. Include "big" and "little" jobs.

2. Make a list of the older people and shut-ins. Set up a program of visitation so they will be visited at least once each two weeks.

3. Have each member see if she cannot find at least one new task which she can do this week.

STOP AND THINK

1. In the light of Matthew 25:31-46 what does Christ feel about "little" and "big" jobs of the Christian?

2. If we are especially fitted for a particular work, what should our attitude be toward preparing for something else?

3. In what ways can making a Christian home be considered as a work of the church?

4. Why do you think women are more suited for benevolent work?

5. Discuss the difference between "finding the time" and "making the time" for some Christian task.

6. What is the best way for finding out what we are able to do?

7. How can we best develop our abilities in serving God.

8. How can hospitality serve more than just a social purpose?

9. If we use the trial and error method of finding our place, what should our attitude be toward our failures?

10. What attitudes can cause all our labor to be ineffective?

THE PREACHER'S WIFE AND THE MISSIONARY WIFE

It was their anniversary. She had spent the afternoon preparing his favorite meal. As the time drew near for him to come home, she hurriedly fed the children, bathed them and tucked them in bed. Putting on her prettiest dress, she began to set the table with her best linen. The phone rang and she went to answer it, with a small feeling of uneasiness creeping into her heart. It was her husband. "Hello, hon! I won't be able to get home for quite some time. Sister Jones called and asked me to meet them at the hospital. Joe is being taken there directly from the plant. He's been injured. Keep supper for me and I'll be home just as soon as I can. Bye."

The scene was taken from real life in a minister's home and we are happy to be able to report that the young wife, though disappointed, put the dinner on the back of the stove. Leaving the table set for a very late meal, she went to her desk and started work on the preparation of a Bible class lesson for Sunday. When the husband finally arrived home with the good news that Joe would be alright, the wife warmed up the dinner and together they sat down to celebrate their anniversary. No word of complaint, no nagging, no self-pity. This was part of her life and because she loved both Christ and her husband, she had learned to accept the problems which come with being the wife of a preacher.

Not all women in this position have matured to such a point. They allow themselves to become mired in self-pity and this will begin to eat into their family life and, of course, will affect the work to which their husbands have chosen to give their lives. Where does the blame lie? Why should these wives feel this way? These are the questions which will have a different answer with each individual. But some of the causes are general and well-recognized. These will be the areas we will cover in this chapter. This study is not intended to be psychiatric in nature but as the title of this book indicates, it is to serve as a gentle admonition to give our lives to better things.

We would not have you think that the wife of a preacher is any different from other wives; she is not. She, like her other Christian sisters, has chosen the man she loves and to whom she entrusted her life. They were married and began establishing their home. The wife of a minister faces the same perplexities which any other woman will face under the same circumstances. Her position in regard to her husband is the same. He is the head over her and she must love and respect him. Theirs is no special relationship in comparison with other marriages. She must strive to build a Christian home, be a good companion to her husband and bring up their children in God's way. But most every occupation brings its own specific problems to the wife, and the ministry is no exception.

PREPARATION FOR MARRYING A PREACHER. Perhaps this has a strange sound to it but if we will study this just a while, we will be able to see that a certain kind of life would serve as adequate preparation for being a preacher's wife. It is sad, but true, that a great many mothers today do not want their daughters to marry an evangelist. The world has become so materialistic that we feel our security is based on the multitude of possessions we pile up around ourselves. We let this attitude creep into our lives and our daughters begin to feel that marriage to a man who has chosen to proclaim God's word cannot offer very much to her. Not many preachers are wealthy in the goods of this world; most of them are inadequately paid for their work. And as mothers, we want our daughters to have nice things and enjoy a good living. We may not even realize that we are teaching our girls that we don't want them to choose a preacher because we may not recognize the fact that we even feel this way. But our actions speak quite loudly and we may not be rearing our daughters in a way that would even make them successful wives to a minister. Luke 12:15 tells us that a "man's life consisteth not in the abundance of the things which he possesseth." We say we believe this but our way of life may prove differently. We should train our daughters in such a way that whether their future mate is rich or poor, she will be prepared to meet and accept the challenges each would present.

The best preparation for marrying a minister is living a godly life. We might add this is the most adequate provision for any marriage. But more especially so if the one whom we choose to marry has given his life to the service of God. We will be acquainted with the responsibilities which God requires of all Christians and if our training has been good, we will have already fulfilled some of those responsibilities. If we love God and His Son and let them reign in our lives, then we can more perfectly meet the challenges which confront us as the wives of preachers. Godly love is always pliable enough and bountiful enough to take in another person. We have loved God first; now we are ready to include a mate in that love.

THE PREACHER'S WIFE MUST SHARE THE LOVE OF HER HUSBAND. This has been the cause of much friction to the preacher's wife. It is human for a young girl to want to be the sole object of affection and attention for the young man she marries. The preacher's wife is no different but her husband's love — on the purest, spiritual level — has already been given to God and His work. This does not mean that his wife is not the queen of his heart nor the dearest person on earth to him. It means that his life's work is a commitment of love and as such, distinguishes this calling from any other occupation. Any wife might feel jealous of the attention her husband gives to his work, but no other profession is in exactly the same category as the ministry. A man should love his trade but it is not the same kind of love which makes the preacher choose his calling above all others; for it contains a close relationship with heavenly love, the most perfect kind. So the wife of such a man must know from the beginning that she must share the heart of her husband with God, and His will, and His work.

THE PREACHER'S WIFE MUST SHARE THE TIME OF HER HUSBAND. It seems to be the common lot of preachers' wives to be alone a great deal of the time. The work of her husband demands odd hours and extra long work days. He may be called out in the middle of the night and she will be alone for many hours, waiting anxiously for his return. He will be out of town holding meetings, raising funds for a special work, or attending a workshop or lectureship. Most of the time she will not be able to go with him. His life must include the problems of others, as well as those of their own home. He may be called upon to counsel another when his wife feels she needs the same comforting advice.

There will be times when the husband will have to be at business meetings of the congregation and she will have another evening alone. If he is active in leading souls to Christ, he may have several cottage classes going at the same time. Another solitary night! These are the times which so often bring despair to the preacher's wife. Yet her role is not so different from that of other wives of busy executives. And she should remember that she is not the only wife who sits alone at home. She must not blame her position in life for this. In speaking to a group of ministers' wives, a psychiatrist said, "You must exercise caution and not blame your role for qualities that do not rightfully belong to it." Don't place the accusation on "being a preacher's wife" for it is the ordinary complaint of wives whose husbands love their work and devote their time and energy in seeing it prosper. Learn to accept this limitation of time together. And certainly make sure that the time you do have is spent in peace and harmony, not nagging over what might have been.

Because your husband must be gone much of the time, you have more freedom in enriching your own life. Perhaps you could take on another activity which you could perform in those long hours of solitude. Reading and study could fill much of that time or why not try your hand at writing if you've never done so? Use your time constructively for Ephesians 5:16 warns us all to "redeem the time." We cannot afford to waste any and you have been blessed with some special time when the children are in bed and your husband has not come home. Learn to accept your own company and enjoy it, for after all you will be spending many, many hours with yourself.

THE PREACHER'S WIFE LIVES ON DISPLAY. In this sense she is a special person for the congregation looks to her as being a good example. I hasten to say that it does take an unusual woman to stand up under the scrutiny of so many people without fleeing from the spotlight thrust upon her at all times. Christians should not expect more from the wife of their minister than from any other Christian woman. To do so is unkind and unnecessary for each should be judged on her own merits and not by some measuring standard which the world has set for preachers wives. But in the system of life as we know it, these women are put under microscopic examination, with suitable praise and usually uncalled for criticism. This is something which the wife will have to face and learn to live with. It is not right, but there are many situations of life which are unjust but which we must nevertheless learn to accept and make the best of. The woman who can live in this merciless (most of the time) spotlight and present a righteous life, smiling and calm, deserves many stars in her crown. Holding fast to God's hand and seeking courage in His love and promises will help carry her through victoriously. I firmly believe that heaven will be made more complete by the presence of a host of these wonderful women and I shall want to meet and know every one of them!

THE PREACHER'S WIFE MUST LIVE WITH CRITICISM — JUST AND UNJUST. People in all walks of life that thrust them in the forefront of the public eye will naturally draw criticism. Some of it will be constructive and as such will be valuable to the person who accepts it. On the other hand, a large part of it will be unjust and even destructive. The preacher's wife must learn to face and live with both, for in choosing the ministry, her husband has placed their family in the focal point of the congregation. And human nature being what it is, even Christians involve themselves in attitudes which are not becoming and above all, not acceptable to God. Yet because personalities are involved in living and worshiping together, criticism will come and sometimes, quite often.

If the criticism is kind and meant to be helpful, she must learn to take it and use it. Her eternal destiny could very well depend upon it. One of the prime purposes of the word of God is reproof, or constructive criticism (I Timothy 3:16). If the person loves us and means well, then our attitude must be one of gratefulness and compliance with the advice.

If the criticism is undeserved, it will naturally cut quite deeply. Yet this too, is a part of life and we must learn to utilize even the bad things which come our way. These are the things which, if endured patiently, will gain us reward. "My brethren, count it all joy when ye fall into divers temptations; knowing this, that the trying of your faith worketh patience. But let patience have her perfect work, that ye may be perfect and entire, wanting nothing" (James 1:2-4). Indeed such cruel words do try our faith and it is only with God's help that we keep ourselves under control. For this is what we must do. We cannot indulge in the immediate desire to "bite" back, returning evil for evil. We must patiently endure and with the assistance of His strength we can do just this, bringing our faith to perfection.

So many of the problems facing the preacher's wife are caused by the congregation expecting too much of her. They seem to feel for some unexplained reason that they "own" her and should thus have some authority over her. If the congregation furnishes a home for the preacher's family, the group seems to think they "own" that home and come and go at their own pleasure. Or they try to tell the wife how she should care for her home and family. This situation should not be allowed because of the discord it brings. If necessary, the elders should see that the congregation respect the privacy of the minister's house. Just because the rent is paid by the church does not give the individual members any authority over its operation. If the house is near the church building, the problems are multiplied. It may became essential for firm steps to be taken in order that the members do not use the house as a social hall, coming and going as they please.

But in all of this, the preacher's wife will be the one who has to tolerate this thoughtlessness. Her life will not be easy but then God has not promised us the "easy way." She may take steps to insure the sanctity of her home but these should be kind, careful and executed in a prayerful attitude. Other women would not tolerate such a situation to exist in their homes and we should not expect the preacher's wife to sit passively and endure such inconsideration on the part of other Christians.

There are not enough appropriate words to praise this great body of women who have loved and married preachers. I believe their rewards will be immeasurable because of the beauty of their lives. Doing without while other women have new clothes. Driving a car (the few times her husband isn't using it) which is older than almost everyone else's. Taking responsibilities which no one else will shoulder. Being criticized for some unjust reason. Moving from place to place and seldom having her *own* house. Sharing her husband's time with others who often impose upon him. Doing a major share of the work of the congregation and seldom receiving any praise. These are just a few of her attributes. She is unpaid, unsung and too often, unloved by the critical. But she is secure in the knowledge that she is loved by her good husband, her wonderful children and above all, she *knows* that God cares for her. This is what makes it all worthwhile.

THE MISSIONARY WIFE. The wife of the missionary is, of course, the wife of a preacher. Everything we have said previously applies to her. Yet the life her husband has chosen in preaching the gospel will bring a diversity of problems her "stay-at-home" sisters do not face. The wife of one of our missionaries said that "living in a foreign country was sometimes like living in a goldfish bowl." Because she will have to face situations unlike anything she has ever known, the woman who goes abroad with her husband must learn to make many adjustments. She should stand ready to accept the new and the different and she should be prepared to be looked upon as something "new and different" by the people of the country where the family goes to work for the Lord.

Each December the *Christian Woman* magazine devotes its articles to the mission field, its families and its work and rewards. I have kept all the issues of this dear little periodical for several years and from the December copies I have taken most of the material used in presenting this theme on the missionary wife. I cannot list here the names of all the women who wrote the many articles but they will know who they are. Many of them are still in the foreign mission fields; some have returned to work here in this country. I humbly and gratefully acknowledge the help of these authoresses who have written for the December issues of *Christian Woman*. I recommend this magazine to those who are not acquainted with it. I respect its editors and the many others who work on it. For a time I was able to serve as associate editor to Bettye Nichols. During this time I learned much about the art of publishing and gained much, much more in my reading acquaintance with the wonderful Christian women who took the time to contribute the articles. Without the help of these publications, I would have had a more difficult time in preparing this section on the wife of the missionary. I can only say, "Thank you."

THE MISSIONARY WIFE MUST COUNT THE COST AND BE ASSURED OF RIGHT MOTIVE. When a young girl takes the marriage vows with her husband, she cannot always see where these will take her. If her mate has chosen to be a missionary preacher, her life will be rich and full, but it can also present difficulties which she must learn to surmount. If she cannot accompany her husband with wholehearted enthusiasm and accord with his work, then the progress of the Lord's church will be definitely hindered. The woman who must help make the decision to go abroad to serve must first count the cost of evaluating her motive. Is she going for the right reason? The love of God and the love of winning lost souls to Christ must be the force that will prompt her to say "Yes, I am ready to serve by your side wherever you want to go." Love for her husband is necessary and will help her over many rough spots in the time that lies ahead. But there should be another, stronger force than this which urges her to accept the challenge. Her husband will be very busy and she will have little time with him. That is why her love for God is so important for this is what will sustain her when she is alone in a foreign country and her husband's love seems so remote when his time is fully occupied with the work of the church.

Most supporting congregations want to interview the wife of the man who is seeking financial help. The elders know that if the wife is not altogether sold on the project, the chances will be for the man to return to the States before he has accomplished much. God expects us to be wise stewards of our money and the elders do not feel it wise to "invest" the congregation's money in an effort which depends to a large extent upon the lukewarm feeling of the wife. Or they may feel that she is going along for a lark, getting a free trip abroad. This sounds callous but has proven true in some cases. The elders want to know that the wife is not only ready and eager to go, but that she is capable and willing to work on her own.

THE MISSIONARY WIFE SHOULD PREPARE TO SERVE. The wife is not taken along for the ride just because her husband is going. She should be a part of the team. There is much she can do which her husband will not be able to undertake. Many opportunities will come for which she will be more suited. And she should be prepared to accept them. If the decision to go is made while the husband is still preparing himself, the wife will have more time in which she can train herself to serve more capably. Perhaps her schooling has prepared her for nursing. This is especially valuable if the choice is to go to one of the under-developed nations of the world. But such specialized training may not be possible. There are other areas for which she can ably fit herself. She can become better acquainted with the office and clerical needs of a congregation. For some time she will probably serve in that capacity in the new work. She can spend time in learning the best ways to keep records, write letters, and put out reports. And most assuredly, she will be training herself to be a better teacher! This is the purpose for which she is leaving all that she is familiar with and traveling thousands of miles away. To go inadequately prepared would be akin to going to battle without any protection of weapons or armor. Many teaching opportunities will be hers and she should be ready to take them.

Another area of service which the missionary wife can prepare for is learning the language of the country to which they are going. In some cases this may not be possible but if it is, then the effort should be put forth. Time will be extremely precious when they reach the new work and if a lot of it has to be spent in learning how to communicate with the people, progress will be slowed to a snail's pace. It is always best to have some knowledge of the language before going.

If the missionary family has children, the wife must also be prepared to teach them in secular classes as well as Bible classes. There may be no schools for them to attend and this responsibility will fall upon the mother. This is a duty to the children because it will affect their lives if they miss out on schooling and have to be held back when they return to America. In most cases you would know prior to going whether there will be education facilities. If there will not be, a lot of your time will be spent in feeding the minds of your children as well as their bodies.

THE TASK OF DAILY LIVING IN A FOREIGN COUNTRY MUST NOT DISCOURAGE. Most Americans, being used to the luxuries which we have come to regard as necessities, find it difficult to adjust to the problems confronting them in a place where these *necessities* are not even considered luxuries — they are unheard of. These things, if encountered with the wrong attitude, can press us into a box of discouragement and disappointment. We must remember that we are in this place to make Christians, not Americans of the people. We will be the foreigner and a novelty to the neighbors, hence the "living in a goldfish bowl" feeling. We will have to learn how to market in a new way. We may have to boil all our water before using it. There may be no handy hot water tank to provide us with the warm bath we need. There might not even be a tub around even if we had some hot water. Our dress, or perhaps the color of our skin may attract attention. The people may want to touch us, our children or our possessions. All these things we should take in stride if we love the souls of those people enough. And like Paul, we can try to be "all things to all people" in order that we might teach them the truth.

THE MISSIONARY WIFE SHOULD BE FRIENDLY AND HOSPIT-ABLE. Marie Cline Hall, writing in the December, 1963, issue of *Christian Woman* gives hospitality a top place in characteristics of the woman in a mission field. Cooking meals for visitors is a frequent job and one which impresses many natives with your friendliness and concern for them. The missionary's house usually stands open to all who feel the need of a haven — for an hour or a night. Sister Hall states that she feels they entertained "angels unawares" many times by inviting the good people they met into their home. She also wrote that another item you should take with you is a *listening ear*. This is good in any country. The good listener is a most valued person. People like to have someone listen to them. Whether it is a joy to be shared or a sorrow to be comforted, learning to listen will serve you in good stead. The friendly, gracious open-hearted woman will do much to further the work of the church in any area of the world where she may be. A sincere smile is a universal language and will serve as a line of communication when words may be a barrier.

The cry of "Go, preach" is being heard by more and more of our evangelists. Every year sees a greater number of preachers and their families journeying to all the lands of the world, heeding the call to teach the nations. In this age of modern communication and travel, we shall probably see the number of missionaries increased even more. This means we should be preparing our young girls to be the wives of these dedicated gospel preachers. We should teach them to meet this challenge with an open heart, ready to go where God has the need. And in the words of Marie Hall, "If we will fill all the corners of our suitcases with *love* and then lock the locks with *courage*, we can be on our way."

SPECIAL ASSIGNMENTS

1. Prepare a list of missionaries' wives. See that each class member is assigned one and ask that a correspondence be started, writing at least once a month. These names can be obtained from many of the Christian publications. This correspondence might be kept in a special scrapbook.

2. Have the class take on a special project of supplying elementary teaching needs to a missionary wife.

3. Have someone make a special study and report on the foreign mission work of the church at the present time. If your congregation supports a foreign work, use this as the basis of the report.

STOP AND THINK

1. Discuss some personality traits which would admirably suit a woman to be the wife of a preacher.

2. How can jealousy on the part of the wife hinder the preacher's work?

3. How can "materialism" lessen the number of young girls who would marry ministers?

4. In the light of this, what should be the attitude of the congregation in setting a salary for the preacher?

5. How can members of the congregation help lighten the load of the preacher's wife?

6. Why should the wife be interviewed when the husband is seeking support for mission work?

7. To most effectively reach the natives of a foreign nation, what should the standard of living be for the American preacher?

8. Why should the motive for choosing to go overseas be so important?

9. Since discouragement is such a common occurence among our foreign missionaries, how can we at home best serve these brethren?

10. Why do you feel there are not more missionaries in the field?

THE WIVES OF ELDERS AND DEACONS

For three times in less than a week, she had been forced to re-arrange their schedule. Each time a call from some member of the congregation took her husband away from their intended activity. As she dressed in preparation for a concert, she almost sensed that the phone would ring again. Downstairs her husband sat waiting for her. He called out, "Better hurry; we don't have too much time." Putting on her hat, she picked up her bag and gloves and turning off the bedroom light, she went down the steps to meet him. Together they walked out the door and got into the car. As they drove to the auditorium she thought to herself, "I'm not selfish with his time, but how good it is to be going some place together."

This was one of her treasured times — times when their evenings were not interrupted with urgent calls from other Christians needing his help. She loved him and did all she could to uphold him in his work for the Lord. The meetings, the calls — these were all part of that work. She was grateful for the time they could spend together but she knew he was filling a position which placed him in the spotlight of being needed by others. He was an elder and when he accepted that office she became a partner to that work. She remembered how they had prepared themselves to fit the roles which they filled. In accepting her husband as one of their elders, the congregation had also revealed their trust in her to fulfil her place as his wife. She had prayed that God would make her fit for this position and now that she had it, she could only be humble and grateful. To share her husband was one way to show her love for God. She could do no less than this.

To be the wife of an elder or deacon should be the goal of every Christian woman. The qualifications which equip a man to be an elder or a deacon are the highest marks of Christian maturity. To be fitted as the wife of one of these men would naturally show the same areas of growth in a woman. And since every Christian is commanded to grow in the "grace and knowledge of our Lord and Savior Jesus Christ" (II Peter 3:18), woman should be training herself to achieve the goals which would make her a suitable wife for an elder or deacon.

To look at some of these wives, we might think they were *born* to the position. They have such poise, dignity and strength of character, moving assuredly through times of joy or sorrow. Yet this is not true. These worthy women are *made*, nor born, for the life they so ably fill. It is a goal within the reach of every woman whose husband is a Christian. Just as each man should be preparing himself to serve in the capacity of elder or deacon, the young woman at his side is working to fit herself as the proper wife. It is well to note at this point, that the qualifications given for the work of elders and deacons in Timothy and Titus are almost identical with the instructions given to all Christians for achieving spiritual maturity. The only exceptions to this are the conditions relating to the material and parental status. Read the passages given in I Timothy 3:1-13 and Titus 1:5-7. Compare these qualities with those given in Romans 12, Colossians 3, Philippians 4 as well as many others. These are mature attributes which we should all strive for, but before a man can be an elder, he must have mastered them to a greater degree. A man does not occupy the position of an elder or deacon on the assumption that he will develop the necessary qualifications. Paul tells Timothy that a bishop, or elder, *must be* certain things. These are not *maybe* or *perhaps* conditions. They are positive traits which the man must attain to a higher degree than others. It would of necessity follow, then, that to be acceptable wives for these men, the women must also have achieved certain qualities. We will be discussing some of these as our lesson progresses. In reality, the life of an elder's or deacon's faithful wife is but the full ripe fruit of Christianity. She is the product of years of self-discipline in controlling her thoughts, guarding her words and restraining her actions. Any Christian woman should seek this worthy goal of Christian maturity, whether or not her husband is chosen to fill one of these offices.

I Timothy 3:11 gives the only direct qualifications for these wives. "Even so must their wives be grave, not slanderers, sober, faithful in all things." The other necessary attributes are gained from a study of the traits which would make her husband suited for the work of either an elder or deacon. We shall take a look at these also.

SHE MUST BE GRAVE. The word used here denotes a dignity of character, a serious manner of speech and a sedateness of action. All this must be evident in the wife of an elder or deacon. She must be *disciplined* in every aspect of her life, having learned to control her thoughts, words and deeds. Her attitude should be one that would draw out the lonely, present trust to the confidant and give a weight of wisdom in any advice she might give. She takes herself and her position in life seriously and is not given to frivolity and childish, raucous behavior. Maturity rests becomingly on her and she has learned to accept her own limitations as well as those of others. She expects the best of herself and those she deals with, but she is never guilty of demanding more than either can give.

SHE MUST NOT BE A SLANDERER. These words carry with them the caution against using her words in a way as to harm or destroy the work of her husband. A slanderer goes about chattering constantly, passing on false reports with the malicious intent of hurting the reputation of someone. The wife of an elder or deacon cannot be this sort of person. Her words will be chosen wisely and used kindly. Henry Delaune once said, "Think all you speak, but speak not all you think. Thoughts are your own; your words are so no more." This woman will not let her words be hurtful to others. She knows that once said, they cannot be "unsaid." Therefore she sets a guard on her lips which places a seal on even a mild insinuation about another. The only qualities of another which she will discuss will be the positive, uplifting ones. In this way, she cannot be the starting point for rumors nor the carrying agent for such poison. She cannot indulge in the sin of gossip because she loves other people and will do nothing to harm them.

Sins of the tongue seem to plague womankind the most. It is a difficult thing to learn how to control this little member of the body, yet James tells us that if we do not bridle our tongue, our religion is vain (James 1:26). This writer of inspired word had a great deal to say about our speech and the use of words. It would be well for women to make special study of his admonition. The Rotary Club of America prints in its membership booklet a warning about the speech its members should use. It advises each one to think before speaking and ask three questions concerning what they desire to say. "Is it the truth?" "Is it helpful?" "Is it necessary?" If it passes these barriers, then it might be safely allowed to enter the world of sound. For once the words pass from our lips, they no longer belong to us. They will have gone out to the good — or detriment — of those who hear them.

SHE MUST BE SOBER. This is translated *temperate* in one version and this more aptly pictures the quality. Again this returns to the thought of self-discipline or self-control, moderation in all things. The woman cannot be moderate until she has learned to curb the different aspects of her life — whether it be food or speech. The dictionary describes the temperate person as one who does not go to extremes. This is what our woman must be. She is neither too enthusiastic nor too mild; she does not run to excess in anything, food, speech, dress, actions or temper. As the wife of an elder or deacon, she must not allow herself to become involved in heated differences of opinion. She will remain calm in the face of such controversy. Even though she might be sore provoked, she will "bear all things, that we may cause no hindrance to the gospel of Christ" (I Corinthians 9:12). She cannot afford to be a party to these disagreements because in so doing, she has involved her husband. He might not be able to take the same position she defends and this could cause friction between the couple as well as in the congregation.

Temperance on the part of the wife would include her manner of dress. Peter gives some explicit commands to every Christian woman as to her adornment in I Peter 3:3-4. These scriptures do not teach against dressing attractively, but they are to serve as a warning that we do not make our clothing the most important thing in our life. Our life should be noteworthy because of the ornament of "a meek and quiet spirit" and not of the fine apparel which we might be able to wear. If people notice and remember us solely because of our dress, then we are failing to present the proper adornment in the eyes of both the world and God. The wife of an elder or deacon must take care that she uses temperance in her clothing. She will be dressed modestly and appropriately but never in a gaudy, too expensive way. In a manner, she stands in a "spotlight" to the other women in the congregation and her mode of attire can serve as a detriment or a positive influence. She will be clothed suitable to her income but always within the best taste and appropriateness for the occasion.

The final admonition in I Timothy 3:11 is an exhortation to be faithful in all things. This faithfulness demands an attitude of sturdy convictions, standing for God's truth in every act of life. The wife of an elder or deacon must maintain her trust and belief in God and her life will give evidence of this to the world. She will be truly "seeking first the kingdom of God and His righteousness."

The qualifications for elders and deacons listed in the two passages given in the beginning of this chapter throw a great deal of light on what kind of women their wives must be. Many of these traits can be achieved by a man only with the cooperation of his mate. For this reason, a study of these conditions for these officers will be of interest and value in determining the qualities of the wife.

WILLINGNESS TO SERVE. The man who accepts the office of an elder must desire the position. He has prepared himself and is now ready and willing to serve His Lord in this way. But the attitude of his wife will have influenced his desire to a great extent. The wife must herself be willing to let him serve. This will mean she will have to share his time, his love, his attention. If she does not stand ready to give in this unselfish way, her husband's willingness alone could not qualify him. He will have to have her support in many ways before he can efficiently and adequately serve as an elder.

HOSPITABLE. It would be almost impossible for a man to qualify in this point unless his wife were at his side. The home is the place where hospitality is usually shown and if the wife does not share her husband's desire to open their home in a cordial welcome, the man can do little to be hospitable. The woman must keep her home prepared for visitors — either for meals or lodging. She will probably keep her pantry stocked with a special "spur-of-the-moment" shelf where she will keep preparations for meals that can be prepared hastily. She stands ready to make a bed available for a visiting preacher or to prepare the living room for a business meeting. She will learn to keep a supply of cookies which can be easily and quickly prepared. Such light refreshments are needed when the meetings are over or when some member drops in for a talk with her husband. She will not be grudging with her hospitality. She will be certain that it is extended without partiality to all the members of the congregation. It will be shown in a spirit of enjoyment and love, keeping in mind that she could very well be entertaining "angels unawares."

NOT GREEDY OF FILTHY LUCRE. This qualification deeply involves the wife also. The socioligists of our day state that the man who is insatiably driven to make money, is usually being pushed by a wife who wants more than his normal income will provide. The elder's wife will have learned to live within their income, being satisfied with what he can provide for her. She will not constantly be purchasing clothing, appliances or furnishings for the home which will bind them financially. She will not be guilty of "pushing" her husband so that he must strive ceaselessly to obtain a better position or to make more money. If these come as a natural matter, she will be grateful for them. But she will not be the cause of her husband being too concerned with making money.

RULER OF OWN HOUSE. We can readily see that a man could not be acceptable in this area if his wife did not recognize the proper position of authority which God has ordained. A man cannot rule if the wife is not subject to him. Therefore an elder's wife must be willing to accept her God-given place beside her husband. She will not try to take his power of authority away from him. He will be the ruler of the home and she will abide by his decisions. Her life will be centered around doing what will bring honor to her husband and to God. She will not try to "boss" or "henpeck" him for in so doing, she has violated the rule set down in the beginning. A man cannot qualify as an elder if his wife dominates him and controls the home. Woman cannot be acceptable to God if she fits this pattern.

It is likewise true that the father cannot have his children in subjection without the aid and support of his wife. Her attitude can undo any positive training he might give them. Both mother and father must agree on the method to be used in raising their children in the nurture and admonition of the Lord. Then the father will administer this policy, while the mother serves as his assistant. The mother can make the father more important and respected by her attitude toward him. She will never be guilty of tearing him down to the children but she will always build him up in their sight. She will share the responsibility of training and discipline and she will help him take his part of this responsibility also. If an elder is to have control of his children, his wife must accept her role in bringing this about.

GOOD REPORT FROM WITHOUT. The man may be of sterling quality and reputation in the community but this alone would not serve to qualify him if his wife did not also possess such a good character. The wife must act at all times in a manner which cannot bring slander upon her husband and the church. She will keep herself clean from gossip and friendships which would entangle her in unsavory situations. Her husband must be able to trust her and she will conduct herself in a way which will show the world that she is trustworthy.

There are other passages given in the New Testament concerning elders and their work. These, too, are necessary to study if we get the complete picture of the kind of woman suitable as their wives. Several times the elders are admonished to "know the flock" over which they have been made overseers. In this age of large congregations, this is sometimes quite difficult to do. But the wife can play an important part in seeing that her husband does get acquainted with the members of the congregation. Because the traits which qualify him to be an elder automatically signify that he has been with the congregation for some period of time, the elder usually knows most of the membership when he is appointed. If he does not, then his wife can make opportunities whereby these unknown families are invited into their home. I have known elders and their wives who make certain each new member is asked to their home for a meal within a short time after placing membership. Often the elder's wife can make more personal visits than her husband. In this way she will become more intimately acquainted with the members and can help her husband know them better. She will probably know of their problems even before he will. This seems to be the nature of woman — to sense the difficulties which others have. When she is aware of such problems, she not only can help relieve them herself but she can assist her husband in knowing the details surrounding such concern. If an elder does not know a large number of the members of the congregation, it is usually an indication that his wife is not as friendly and hospitable as she should be. The final responsibility to know and understand "his flock" rests with the elder, but his wife can help lighten this load.

One of the most important things an elder's wife must face is that she will not be able to share certain "secrets" which her husband possesses. His work is often of a confidential nature and as such, he cannot divulge the details even to his own wife. These burdens are his alone to bear, along with the help of God. The wife must be understanding in this, realizing that it is not to the best interest of the Lord's work for her to be "in" on everything which the elders know and do. This is difficult but her husband is not doing this to shut her out. These special confidences have nothing to do with their relationship as man and wife and therefore, she must not feel jealousy because she does not share them.

Every qualification which we have discussed applies to each Christian woman who is seeking to fit her life into the mature, acceptable pattern God desires. Yet because the wife of an elder or deacon has a role which places her in a position of more influence, her responsibility is even more serious. Their husbands are the examples, the leaders, the ones who must answer for the souls under their care. For this reason, we must acknowledge the degree of responsibility falling on their wives as being greater because of the more public nature of their role. If the wife fails to share the love of her husband in every good thing and does yield to her own selfish wishes, she can not only lose her own soul, but she could possibly cause her husband to stumble also. If this does happen, it could very well mean the loss of many he is duty-bound to oversee and guide. The wife must look well to her life and see that she cannot be charged with this awesome indictment. If our husbands are called upon to serve as elders, or deacons, let us not be the cause of their replying, "I have married a wife, and therefore I cannot come" (Luke 14:20).

SPECIAL ASSIGNMENTS

1. Have someone make a chart of the qualifications of elders and deacons and put beside each if and how the wife can help her husband qualify.

2. Prepare a lesson and spend one class period on the sins of the tongue as shown in the book of James.

3. If your congregation has elders, ask one of them to speak to the class on "The Value of a Good Wife to the Elder."

STOP AND THINK

1. Why is preparation on the part of the wife so important in the eldership?

2. Can the qualifications of elders and deacons completely exclude the wife? Why?

3. If the qualifications for these offices are almost identical with other Christian maturity conditions, what makes it more necessary that these men be equipped with these traits to a greater degree than the membership?

4. Since the Bible tells us that no man is perfect, how can a man qualify in all of these conditions and still be imperfect?

5. Why would the giddy, "social butterfly" not be suitable to be the wife of an elder or deacon?

6. Do you feel a man can be hospitable if his wife does not possess this trait? How?

7. Why should these wives be careful about only one "best" friend?

8. Since self-control seems to be the keynote of the lives of godly women, discuss the areas of life which must be disciplined.

9. Do you feel the elders' wives should dress in standard far above that of the rest of the congregation even if she can afford it?

10. How can a congregation have a "woman elder?" (Notice quotation marks) Discuss the qualifications which this would violate.

CHAPTER IX

THE BUSINESS WOMAN

She had left home fifteen minutes late this morning. When she reached the office, the clock showed her she was behind in her schedule. The activities of the day seemed to prove this point. She had not been able to "catch up" all day and now it was almost quitting time. Racing against the hands of the clock, she kept herself going at a pace which was tightening her nerves and threatening to overwhelm her at any moment. Finally the working day was over and she sat at her desk while her fellow employees said goodbye and left. Her spirit seemed to give up and she slumped in her chair and put her head in her arms on the desk before her. Tears of self-pity welled to her eyes; she was utterly dejected!

She certainly had not felt this way when she had pleaded with her husband to allow her to seek a job. She had seen the neatly groomed women coming from the office building when she came to pick up her husband. How she had envied them! They were living a full, exciting life while she was just existing in the drudge-world of children and housework. She knew now that what she had seen in those working women was only the exterior presented to the world. If she could have seen what went on in many of their minds and their private lives, she would never have been so eager to step into the business world. How good her pre-job life seemed to her now! With determination in her heart she prepared to leave the office. When she reached home she knew what she was going to do. Her husband would be overjoyed to have her back as simply his wife and the mother of his children. She could hardly wait to give her two weeks' notice and return to the place where she belonged!

This picture of the working woman is not true of every Christian woman who has chosen to exist in the business world as well as the world of the homemaker. Many such women are capable of handling a full time job and still keep their home running smoothly. To some of these, working is a necessity in order that she might support her family. Others are employed in order to meet some financial crisis which faces their husbands. Still others work because they wish to provide Christian education for their children. These are only a few of the worthwhile reasons why woman might choose to combine a career with being a homemaker. You will notice I said "worthwhile" reasons for there are numerous other excuses which too many women use to condone their taking work outside the home.

I want to hasten to say at this point that I am not against a woman working in the world. Until just a few short weeks ago I found myself in that category. I have worked in different capacities under ideal and far from ideal situations. I do not say I am an expert on the business woman but I have gained much from my own experience and will rely on that knowledge in preparing this study on the subject.

The ideal sphere of life for woman is the home. God intended it this way and only a very few would deny the truth of this statement. Yet all of life is seldom ideal and we must recognize the fact that many times woman is faced with the problem of providing the necessities of life for a family left fatherless. Financial problems come to our husbands through no fault of their own and we might be called on to supplement the income. The sad truth is that in facing life and its difficulties, woman might be required to seek employment outside the "ideal" sphere where she was placed.

Then, too, we have the single woman who supports herself through employment in the business world. Either she has not yet married or she has remained single through her own choice. In either case she has become a part of that world outside the home which provides the products or services which make the world operate more smoothly. Her responsibilities to her family may differ from that of the working married woman, but her duties to God and to her employer will be the same. This group of women has much to offer to the church and to the world by their works and influence.

It is the duty and privilege of the Christian woman to be industrious and care for the needs of her home and family. These are her primary functions and as such, hold first place in her time and attention. If she can meet these obligations and still work at another job, then she can feel free to do so. Nevertheless she should keep in mind the fact that broken homes and maladjusted children often add their much greater problems to the existing one which caused her to seek employment in the first place. God has never condemned the working woman and we should not take the authority to do this ourselves. We cannot know the reasons behind such actions and cannot serve as judge of our sister Christians who work. If they can fulfill the roles they have accepted within the framework of God's commands and the examples He has given, then we can do nothing less than take them at the values they present in their lives. After all, we are in no position to accept or reject people on the basis of how many activities they are able to include in their life.

Lydia was perhaps the best example left to us of the business woman. The sixteenth chapter of Acts gives us the story of this dedicated woman. Not only was she working as a seller of purple, but she was also a worshipper of God. Thus we see that being a career woman does not preclude that we cannot worship God. She was zealous and open-hearted (verse 14) and when she heard the truth, she immediately accepted it. Is it not possible that her business life had sharpened her senses to the point where she could detect the best in life? She was evidently successful in business because we can also read of her household and this would mean she was financially able to keep a retinue of servants, as well as possibly some members of her own immediate family. Being an industrious business woman did not keep Lydia from being hospitable for she immediately asked that the apostles come to stay with her. By studying this sixteenth chapter of Acts, we can see that God does not disapprove of a woman working in the business world. Only a close scrutiny of her life and motives might prove her unacceptable.

Before we make the decision to become either the breadwinner or the *assistant* breadwinner, there are some questions which we should evaluate and answer honestly.

IS IT REALLY NECESSARY FOR ME TO WORK? Many times this must be answered with a positive "Yes." Illness of the husband or death of the mate are the usual reasons for such an unqualified affirmative. But even in these circumstances, it is not always an absolute necessity. In case of serious illness, the husband sometimes has unemployment or casualty insurance. Of course, living on a reduced income would be difficult but often the wife could remain at home if she were willing to make the necessary budget adjustments. This is true in the case of death also. The insurance could be set up to provide a monthly income instead of a lump sum benefit which can so easily be used up. Again this would entail a budgetary re-alignment and perhaps even a lower standard of living. But the wife and mother should weigh the advantages of her presence at home carefully against the seeming advantage of having more money. If the income must be supplemented, then she could seek either part time employment or some kind of work that she could perform at home.

There are times when financial obligations press in upon the family to such an extent that it is expedient for the wife to get a job. In situations such as this, it is best that the work sought be of temporary nature so that when the debt problem has been alleviated, the wife can easily quit and return to being just a homemaker. If the employment is of the permanent type, the woman too often will not feel the urge to quit when the temporary necessity is gone. She will remain at work out of a sense of duty to her employer or because she has grown to enjoy this "separate" life and is not willing to give it up.

DO I WORK TO FINANCE SOME LUXURY? America has become so materialistic that we can no longer recognize the difference between a necessity and a luxury. As a result, perhaps we find that we can answer negatively. But a closer look would probably reveal that the new car, house, TV, stereo or whatever it might be can hardly be classed as a necessity. Certainly the husband will appreciate the attitude which causes the wife to want to help gain these niceties of life. But by staying home and learning to budget what *he* makes wisely may help him save the money to make these purchases without taking away the sense of achievement he has as the provider of the family. The husband of a woman who works does not usually have the feeling of being as *good* a provider as the one whose wife remains at home. If a woman works solely to have a higher standard of living, she should search her soul carefully to see if "seeking first His kingdom" has lost its place as her goal in life.

DO I WORK TO SAVE MONEY FOR MY CHILDREN'S COLLEGE EDUCATION? No one denies the worthiness of this purpose. Yet we should look closer before we use it as a reason to seek employment. If our children are all of college age with no little ones left at home, then our working to help them get an education might be a good thing. If we want to see that *they* do not have to work for an education, then our purpose is not so acceptable. They should be ready to help share this load also. Let us look at the mother who is working when her children are small in order that she can put aside all that she earns to insure them a college degree. Has she not forgotten that her children are getting an education *now* and perhaps it is the kind that would take them away from the kind of life she visualizes for them. If they do not have the Christian foundation of training in love, their character will be molded into a foreign pattern and the mother can only wish she had taken a more positive attitude toward forming their way of life. This early training could possibly prove more valuable than any higher scholastic education. This mother, of necessity, will be unable to spend as much time with and for her children. Her purpose is worthy but will her little ones understand it? Probably not. They will only know that she did not have the extra time to give them *now*. Education is excellent and it is wonderful when a person can obtain all they are capable of achieving. But a mother is a better education and the future hope of a college degree seems cold and remote when the child only wants the warm, tender security of his mother's arms to comfort him.

DO I WORK TO FEEL INDEPENDENT OF MY HUSBAND? The woman who has a good job often falls into the trap of feeling independent. It is even possible that she makes more than her husband. This is a ready-made situation for marital disaster! Ephesians 5:23-24 should be pasted on the mirror of every working woman lest she be tempted to move outside its pattern of authority. "For the husband is the head of the wife, even as Christ is the head of the church . . . Therefore as the church is subject unto Christ, so let the wives be to their own husbands in everything." When the feeling of having "her own" money becomes too endearing, the woman is in danger of losing her position as helpmeet to her husband. The best way to handle the financial arrangements when both mates work is a joint affair — not his account and her account. The woman who cannot be subject to her husband in "all" things, and this includes money, should not have married in the first place. A situation involving this feeling of independence on the part of woman almost surely causes the man to lose self-respect and in many cases, will lead to a broken home.

CAN I RUN MY HOME EFFICIENTLY AND STILL HOLD A JOB? Since each of us are given the same twenty-four hours a day in which to live, it is absolutely necessary that our time be budgeted in order that we may accomplish the most. As we take on the added responsibility of an outside job, we must schedule our use of time even more rigidly. Will we neglect our home by letting the housework slip by undone and the laundry pile up? Will my family be well-groomed or will there be buttons missing, un-ironed clothing worn and hems torn out? Will I feel that my husband should take on more of the housework because I am working out? After all, these chores are my responsibility and if I take on another, then I must stand ready to fit all the necessary duties into my time schedule. If my home life suffers, then I should not be working.

When a woman accepts a position, she usually has to give up certain activities related to her family. She can no longer visit the school room on visitation day. Even her voluntary work for the PTA or hospital will have to be rejected. Her association with neighborhood friends usually ceases because she just does not have the time to fit these "extras" into her schedule. She cannot serve as a scout leader or den mother. Her children may be excluded from some activities simply because she will not be able to participate in the work load of organization.

IS MY JOB RESPECTABLE? It would seem that it is unnecessary to speak of this to Christian women. Yet it is possible that some might possibly seek employment in places where the reputation of the family would suffer. The work itself might be honorable but the business be tainted by public moral opinion. It is conceivable that a woman who is not trained for any skilled labor might be employed in a menial occupation. Within itself there is nothing wrong with her work, but it might be detrimental to her husband's position in the community, especially if he is in a professional field. The influence of our husband and family should come before any monetary purpose.

WHO WILL CARE FOR MY CHILDREN? This should be of prime concern to the working mother. If she is not to be on hand to train her children and bring them through the trying years of youth, she must make doubly certain that she is entrusting them to someone whose morals and ideals are the same as her own. The ideal situation would be to find a Christian woman who needs the employment. In this way we can be sure she will guide the children in the way we want them to go. Little minds can be warped and twisted by the ideas planted by adults, and if we are leaving them in the care of someone else, we are taking a risk. We can never know fully what the other person feels and is, and our desire to work might be stronger than our intuition in judging a baby-sitter. This is perhaps the greatest problem facing the working mother. Until it can be solved to the best interest of the child, the mother should never accept employment. No amount of money she might earn could compensate for the loss of that child's soul by improper training.

WILL I STILL DO CHURCH WORK? Every Christian is commanded to "seek first the kingdom of God and His righteousness," and this remains binding whether or not we are employed outside the home. Too many women feel that regular worship attendance is all that is expected of her, especially if she is working five or six days a week. We cannot study the Bible and conclude that this is all we are expected to do. There is teaching to be done; benevolent work to be seen to; many tasks which must be shouldered by someone. Will I still be able to function in an active position in the work of the church? God will not relieve me of these obligations simply because I choose to take on another responsibility.

If I can answer all these questions honestly and satisfactorily, then and only then would it be wise to accept employment. When the decision has been made and after every precaution has been taken to keep the home running smoothly, I must be ready to accept the added responsibilities which will come with working for another person. I have taken the obligation to live "two" lives, so to speak, and I am directly chargeable for both. I have added another area of duty to my Christian life and I must stand ready to discharge my responsibility to each.

MY TIME FROM 8 TO 5 BELONGS TO MY EMPLOYER. When a woman takes a job, she is in reality giving about forty hours of her time each week to her employer. This belongs to him and she has the responsibility to use that time to his best interests. If his business is not our prime concern during the working day, then we have failed to meet our duty. This means I will put forth my best mental capabilities to serve him. I will give equal work for the time purchased from me. If coffee breaks are given, then I will enjoy them within the limits set by my boss. These periods were originally intended to give the workers a few minutes respite from their tasks; to relieve their minds and bodies so they could return refreshed. Many employees have distorted this privilege and as a result have "stolen" time from their employer. If fifteen minutes is alloted, this is what I will take—no more. My lunch periods will be scheduled to fit the needs of the business, not my own personal desires. They will be spent in such a way as to allow me to return to work at the proper time.

Since everyone who works is doing so for the income involved, this is quite important to them. The feeling of having earned our wages is a pleasant one, and if we are living the Christian life, satisfying our employer with our best performance will bring this satisfaction. Too often we begin to feel that we are giving more than we are receiving, and dissatisfaction creeps into our work. We must not have the attitude of doing just enough to get by. Our position should be one in keeping with Colossians 3:23-24. "Whatsoever ye do, work heartily, as unto the Lord, and not unto men; knowing that from the Lord ye shall receive the recompense of the inheritance: ye serve the Lord Christ." We serve another employer—Jesus Christ—and one much more important than any earthly boss. We should be willing to "go the second mile," give more than is expected of us; for we are not only working for the monetary wage we will be paid here, but we look forward to the heavenly inheritance!

MY LOYALTY BELONGS TO MY EMPLOYER, BUT FIRST OF ALL TO CHRIST. I will be faithful to the person who hires me, always seeking his best interests. But my first loyalty remains to Christ and I must never allow any facet of my occupation to reflect upon that loyalty. Any taint of dishonesty cannot be a part of my work. It is possible that such things will be asked of me. I cannot change my character to earn money. It would be better to resign my job. My employer may furnish entertainment for the workers at certain times of the year. If this entertainment is questionable, I cannot participate in it. I will not lie, swear, cheat or accept any other moral defect on my life. I will present the best to my employer and be faithful to him, but Christ is first in my life and it will be evident by my actions that He is the one I am seeking to please (Ephesians 6:5-7).

MY INFLUENCE MUST BE FOR CHRIST. When we moved to the upper midwest several years ago, it was necessary for me to seek employment. There were very few Christians in this part of our nation and none at all in my place of work. Only one of my fellow workers did not smoke, and every one of them drank socially and most of them used language unbecoming a woman (or man, too, for that matter). I felt completely surrounded by worldliness and wondered if I could be strong enough to be a positive influence. It is never easy to stand alone in a crowd and particularly so, when you want the people to like you. I soon learned that my approach had to be quiet, positive and definite. My time was spent in getting my work done, and since the coffee breaks were nothing more than "smoke-gossip" times, I just did not take them. I did not attend the big holiday dances nor did I participate in the cocktail parties given when some employee left. I had to be more positive about the language used around me for I could not bear to hear the name of my Lord used so vainly. Was I considered unusual and perhaps fanatic? I'm sure that I was by some of the women. But I soon learned that most of them respected, and yes, even admired, me for my stand. My boss knew that I would work extra hours if needed and unless something unusual came up, I finished my work before I left for the day. The proof of what kind of employee I made came when I resigned. Each person who had any authority over me wrote extremely kind and complimentary statements on my report. The greatest aid to me during all my employment was prayer! I prayed that my work would be acceptable not only to my employer, but to Christ as well. I prayed that I would serve as an influence for good. I prayed for opportunities to talk with my fellow workers about Christ. Help came in each of these categories. I was not able to win any of my friends at work to Christ, but this I know—more people in that office know about the church of Christ!

The woman in the business world has responsibilities to God, to her family, to her employer, and to herself. This is a full life she has chosen to lead, but it was one of her own choosing. For this reason she has a heavier load of responsibilities. She cannot meet all these without help. "And whatsoever we ask, we receive of him, because we keep his commandments, and do those things that are pleasing in his sight" (I John 3:22). Only a close relationship with God can serve to see her wisely through all her days. Her sphere of influence has widened to include more than the home, family and church. She can do much to aid the work of the Lord and with His help, she will meet each opportunity with a willingness to grasp it and use it to His glory.

SPECIAL ASSIGNMENTS

1. Have some member make a special report on the business qualities of the worthy woman of Proverbs 31.

2. Have some member who is presently working or who has worked in the business world to make a short talk on living the Christian life at work.

3. Prepare a panel discussion lesson on the negative and positive sides of the working woman.

STOP AND THINK

1. What are some "worthy" reasons for women to work?

2. What are some "unworthy" reasons? Why?

3. In view of the passages in Acts 16 and Proverbs 31 concerning women working, what do you feel is God's view on the working woman?

4. What is the usual effect on the husband when the wife holds a more important position than his own? How does this violate God's standard for the husband and wife?

5. In counting the cost of baby-sitters, appropriate clothing, transportation and other necessary costs of a job, do you feel it really is worthwhile for a woman to work?

6. Discuss why early training of children is more valuable than higher education.

7. If the wife works, should the husband and children be expected to take on extra household chores? Discuss.

8. What qualities should the person have to whom you entrust the care of your children while at work?

9. Should the working woman be excused from accepting responsibilities in the work of the church?

10. How can we be loyal to both Christ and our employer?

CHAPTER X

THE CITIZEN

It was election day. It was also hot, humid and extremely uncomfortable. The young mother stood waiting in line at the polling place. Two small children were by her side and she carried a baby in her arms. The line to the voting machines was quite long and the time passed into thirty minutes, then forty-five. The children grew restless and one began to fret and cry. Some of the others in the waiting group wondered how the young mother could stand so patiently in such miserable circumstances. An older woman walked to her and said, "Why do you wait in line for such a long time just to vote? It's hot and your children are cross and tired. Maybe you could come back later."

The young woman shifted the baby in her arms and comforted the fretful child at her side. Her voice was soft, patient, and showed a touch of foreign accent. Looking into the eyes of the questioner she said, "I must vote now. You see, this is the first time I have ever been allowed to help select who will rule over me. In the old country we had no choice. Now I am a naturalized American citizen and you understand, surely, a citizen must vote." Those who heard her gentle, but firm words could not help but be ashamed of their own irritation at waiting for so long to cast their vote. Suddenly the day was more pleasant and surprisingly, even the line seemed to move faster!

America has come a long way in her relatively short history. Her way of progress and prosperity has attracted the thoughts and dreams of people the world over. Today we are blessed with the privilege of living in the wealthiest nation in all of history. The way of life for even those in poverty is on a higher level than the natives of many foreign countries. We live surrounded by plenty—sitting at our tables with our cup of blessing overflowing. Yet how many of us ever think that this flow could possibly stop. We spend a great deal of time talking about our freedoms, yet too many of us do nothing to deserve them.

It has been stated that "America is Americans attempting self-government while situated in a fortunate geographical position." Our nation was founded on a faith in God and a belief in the right of the individual. This is what makes it so unique in a world full of dictators and premiers. It implies that we do not have to have a police state which uses secret agents to force us to obey the laws of the land—but it places the responsibility on the individual. Each one should be desirous of doing what is acceptable and right and molding his life accordingly. This individual yearning for peace and proper government unites and becomes this government *by the people.*

Only history in the centuries ahead will be able to record whether our "experiment" was a success (if God allows time to continue for those centuries). I would hasten to say that if it is a failure, the fault will not lie in the concept of government by and for the people. It will have to be blamed on the individuals who were not willing to take the responsibility of their share of the load in this method of rule. Only when the citizens work together as a composite unit—seeking what is right in a God-centered culture, can a nation such as ours realize its full potential of worth and glory.

Because the emphasis is on the individual, this gets right down to us. As American citizens, we are the individuals who make this nation either prosper or fall. As Christians, we should be the best citizens our country could have, for our concept of right fits naturally into the pattern upon which this great nation was founded. Christians must be conscious of their relationship to their government, and the privileges and responsibilities which this brings. As *Christian* Americans we should be vitally interested in this land of ours and seek the place we can fill in shouldering our obligations to keep it free.

THE WAY TO FREEDOM. Ernest H. Cherrington said, "We are accustomed to say that the truth makes men free. It does nothing of the kind. It is the knowledge of the truth that creates freedom." This is confirmed in God's word for John 8:32 states, "And ye shall *know* the truth, and the truth shall make you free." Knowledge of the truth is necessary before freedom takes place. Truth is the streetcar which takes you to freedom but knowledge is the ticket which puts you on that conveyance. So the best way for us to insure that we keep America free, is to *know*—in other words, we must be informed citizenry.

Too many of us do not make the effort necessary to inform ourselves of the issues in any campaign or to know who the candidates are and what they represent. How many times have we faced a ballot with names on it that we have never heard? Do we mark haphazardly by some "eeny, meny, miney, moe" method and then wonder later why that particular office is so poorly run? Or maybe we don't vote at all because don't know the issues at stake or any of the candidates. Perhaps through our negligence the wrong man might get elected. A presidential election several years ago would have had a different outcome had one more person in each precinct of only four states voted for the defeated candidate. So the importance of even one vote cannot be overlooked.

We should take the time to study the campaign promises, the candidates, the issues. Certainly this is not an easy task yet with the modern methods of communication available to us, it is much easier than our grandparents had it. TV, magazines, newspapers—all can give us assistance in selecting the person most ably suited to guide our government. Perhaps if this information were not so accessible, we would seek it out but because it is there and so easily obtained, we tend to neglect it. Our interest should be as high and as informed on local issues as well as the state and national level. Sometimes we think these "little" elections are not very important. Yet we should realize that our lives are touched and affected more readily by these local issues and officeholders. The state and national ones involve us also but on a more indirect basis. In any election, the Christian should make certain he is an informed voter. This involves seeking the candidate or the issue which will more closely fit into the pattern of life which God has set forth for His children.

Being informed about the nation is just as necessary during off-election years. We should include a worthy news magazine in our subscriptions. The newspapers should be read and evaluated to help us know what is going on in our nation and in the world. A citizenry which does not care what is happening or where it is heading has only rocky, dangerous roads ahead. We should be interested in knowing how government works. This can be accomplished by taking part in politics on both the community, state and national levels—attending party caucuses and study groups, visiting legislative bodies, writing letters to our government officials. Many of our children know more about the process of government than we do. And this speaks well for what their generation can be if they remain informed and interested.

THE CHRISTIAN CITIZEN WILL OBEY THE LAWS OF THE LAND. The Christian cannot obey or disobey the law as a matter of personal preference. To disobey civil law is to disobey God. "For there is no power but of God: the powers that be are ordained of God. Whosover therefore resisteth the power, resisteth the ordinance of God" (Romans 13:1-2). Though we cannot always see the purpose of many laws, many governments, or many of the acts performed by some governments, in God's plan they each have a place. And as long as they do not conflict with God's law, then it is our duty to obey the legislation placed upon us. If we do not agree with the law, we still do not have the authority to disobey it if it does not go directly against God's law. In fact, to keep the letter of our laws is to further Christ's cause. "Submit yourselves to every ordinance of man for the Lord's sake" (I Peter 2:13). We are fortunate indeed that we live in a land where the statutes do not interfere with God's law. Yet if they did, we should have to be courageous enough to stand for the divine right. The early Christians were forced to meet in caves when the laws of the land demanded them to cease worshiping God. The apostles preached in direct disobedience to the laws of the ruling men. Today in Poland we have deeply sincere and courageous Christian brethren who meet weekly to worship in defiance of government orders. Some have been imprisoned repeatedly and yet they remain faithful to God's commands. May we pray that America will never see this precious freedom taken away and we, and our children's children will always be free to assemble together to praise and worship God.

There are some laws of the land which too many Christians look upon as "minor" and hence will violate them if they feel they will not be caught. Have you ever been guilty of exceeding the speed limit when you were in a hurry? Have you ever run a stop sight if you saw no other car in sight? What about jaywalking, double parking? Minor things, we say. Yet they are laws of the land and were passed for our best interest. Our neglect to obey these can teach our children a powerful lesson. "If mother does not have to obey, then I don't have to either." "Going five miles over the speed limit must not be so bad if mother does it." We cannot afford to instruct our loved ones in such a negative way.

One of the most disliked ordinances on the records is the income tax law. More grumbling is done about this than perhaps any other statute we are called upon to obey. We complain because we do not have enough deductions; we gripe because the tax is too high. And saddest of all, too many Christians commit the sin of cheating on their report. They will list contributions for which they are not entitled; they fail to include income which might place them in a higher bracket. One Christian man who works for the Internal Revenue Service once stated, "If all the money listed as church donations were actually given, the congregations in this area could support one hundred missionaries." He was also a deacon in one of the large congregations and he knew what their contributions actually were. Would any of us choose to exchange the taxes we pay for a life in a land with no taxes but constant servitude? I think not. Then our attitude should be one of gratefulness that we can enjoy the blessings paid for by taxes—roads, schools, beautiful parks. David would not offer to God a sacrifice which he had not purchased. "I will not offer my God that which cost me nothing." Then we should feel that we cannot enjoy blessings which have cost us nothing. If taxes are the price we must pay for experiencing the life we have here in America, then I, for one, am willing to pay the price! "Render unto Caesar the things that are Caesar's" (Mark 12:17).

THE CHRISTIAN CITIZEN WILL PRAY FOR HIS NATION. Our actions toward our government are not all passive obedience; they include positive duties as well. "I exhort therefore, that, first of all, supplications, prayers, intercessions, and giving of thanks, be made for all men; For kings, and for all that are in authority; that we may lead a quiet and peaceable life in all godliness and honesty" (I Timothy 2:1-2). Let us look at the components of this passage and see just what our obligation is to those in power. First, we are to make supplication for them. This carries with it the meaning that we will make specific requests of God in behalf of those governing. We can come boldly before God's throne seeking a certain blessing. We are next told to offer prayers for those in authority. This prayer is a direct seeking of guidance for these men in high places. It is a powerful thought to understand that we have been commanded to intercede for those in power. I, an ordinary citizen, (not ordinary, really, but a Christian citizen) have been given the privilege of pleading before God for His blessings on the president of my country, the king of another nation and the premier of another. This is a great privilege extended to man and one which we should not use lightly. Of course, this intercession is not valid for the souls of these men; we have not the authority for that. Individually, they must obey God to insure the safety of their souls. My intercession is for divine guidance in ruling the world. The last thing we are commanded is to give thanks for our rulers. Most of them are dedicated individuals, serving the public welfare with little hope of personal remuneration. Why should we do all these things? The reason is given also. "That we may lead a quiet and peaceable life in all godliness and honesty." Our prayers to God for those in authority in this world could very well mean the difference between war and peace—between freedom and bondage for our people.

THE CHRISTIAN CITIZEN WILL SERVE. Not only must we be informed citizens and follow the direct commands of God concerning this role in our life, we must also stand ready to serve in any way which will make our community, our nation a better place. These can never be better than the sum total of the individual citizens of which they are made. And when the individual decides to make his world a better one, he will start with self-evaluation and self-discipline. There are many activities in which the Christian can participate to promote the better life. Each of them will involve time and work and unless we are willing to give these, there is no place for us in community work. First, we might labor in behalf of some particular issue or candidate. Each campaign has need for many volunteer workers who may do "unglamorous" things like stuffing envelopes, licking stamps, or putting up posters. Maybe we have visualized ourselves as defending our stand in some great oratorical debate. We probably will never get the opportunity. But licking a stamp indicates the firmness of our conviction and so does any of the other small jobs. We can have neighborhood coffee parties to introduce our friends to our choice or to discuss the local bond issue which is up for approval. If we really want to serve in the political life of our city, all we have to do is let it be known we are ready, willing and eager. The job will be ours!

We might serve in some civic service which provides for helping people physically or mentally handicapped. There are many schools, homes, therapy centers and hospitals that need volunteer help. The services we perform can never be measured in monetary gain for we are giving ourselves to heeding the call of the sick at heart, the sick of mind, and the sick in body. In many of these opportunities, we will find that *we* are the ones receiving the greatest blessing. In most cities there are worthy financial drives every year to provide for research into the causes and cures for disease. These campaigns are staffed almost entirely through people giving their time to ring doorbells, seek contributions, or give out literature. We can serve these areas also for the aid given such research could well mean the physical welfare of some of our own loved ones.

We may be called upon to serve in the capacity of some official nature—perhaps the planning and zoning board, the library board, movie censorship study board, recreation groups. In accepting such positions, we are placing ourselves in a more influential role for Christ. If we come in contact with more people, then it stands to reason that more people will be influenced by the righteousness of life, as proved by our actions and words in filling the job we have been given.

We could not begin to list all the places where we might serve our community and nation. PTA organizations, scout troups, musical groups, nature preservation activities—all these are worthwhile and deserve our support. We are to do these things ". . . as we have opportunity, let us do good to all men." How? With zeal and cheerfulness (Romans 12:8), in love (I Corinthians 13:3), remembering the Golden Rule (Luke 6:31), without bitterness, wrath, slander, or malice (Ephesians 4:31), and with compassion, kindness, lowliness, meekness, patience, forbearance and forgiveness (Colossians 3:12), always conducting ourselves wisely (Colossians 4:5).

THE CHRISTIAN CITIZEN WILL NOT LOOK TO GOVERNMENT FOR SUPPORT. The prevailing attitude of too many Americans is "let the government do it for us." We seem to feel that we are getting something for nothing when such a handout is given but this could not be further from the truth. The government in this land is made up of the single individual. It is the taxes of these people which finance the projects the government undertakes. If a general give-away is legislated, then we may be certain that increased taxes will not be far behind. We want the government to supply our youths with jobs, our adults with subsidized businesses and our older people with support for the rest of their lives. We are literally asking to be placed in bondage. Does this sound surprising to you?

It has been said that human history revolves in a circle. In bondage, man begins to have faith. With faith, he develops courage. From this courage, he acts to free himself. Having achieved his freedom, prosperity comes. With this plenty, man begins to be selfish, seeking only his own welfare no matter the cost. This selfishness will make him dependent upon the person or government who will support him. From this terrible dependency, man again sinks into bondage. This cycle has repeated itself in the great nations which have risen and then fallen. Governments do not change from good to bad overnight. Their fall is a gradual process. The Roman Empire existed for 200 years after it seemed virtually certain that it was doomed. Just because our great country seems so invincible to us, let us never lose sight of the fact that if the citizens begin to depend upon the government for their welfare and support, America can decline and decay. We only have to look around us to see that more and more legislation is being passed which demands that the government provide the very sustenance of our people. As Christians we must not let this attitude become prevalent.

The Christian must take care of his own through honest labor. If he is unable to do this because of some providential hindrance, then his fellow Christians must rally to his support. It is the duty of the Christian family to take care of its widows, its older people and its orphans. By passing this responsibility to the government, we are not only disobeying God's law but we are giving an invitation for our free way of life to be taken from us.

HOW MUCH TIME CAN I GIVE TO SERVING MY COMMUNITY?

This is a question which cannot be answered for you in exact hours. I do not know your life or the schedule of time which you live by. Each of us will have to answer this for ourselves after prayerful deliberation. We must decide first of all what we feel we can do since none of us could function in all of these activities. After we have chosen the field which interests us most, our next step is to look at our time schedule and see just how much we can give without disrupting our household duties, without making the family feel neglected, and above all, without interfering with or omitting work of the Lord.

Our primary responsibility is to our family and their spiritual growth. This must not be pushed into the background while we accept civic responsibilities. The church must receive our active, loyal support and we cannot take time from His work to give to the community. If our children are young, we will be limited as to the number of activities which we can undertake. If we can accept only one outside duty, then it must be in the Lord's work and not for the public. A happy, relaxed mother will serve the Lord better than the hurried, nervous one. She may not receive the commendation of the world but she can be assured that God's praise will make up for any she might have missed in serving elsewhere.

What America is, depends upon what Americans are. It is conceivable that our nation might not always be the stronghold of freedom which she presents to the enslaved of the world today. If she falls, if she decays and vanishes into bondage we the individual citizen will have to shoulder the blame. It is up to us whether we live in rejoicing or mourning for here in our nation, we, the people, are the government. "When the righteous are in authority, the people rejoice; but when the wicked beareth rule, the people mourn" (Proverbs 29:2).

SPECIAL ASSIGNMENTS

1. Have someone make a list of civic activities which the members might participate in.

2. Have someone make a special report on the influence of God in the formation of our government.

3. Prepare a short quiz on local government in your city and some of its recent problems (just 4 or 5 questions). See how well informed the class is. This would be a self-evaluation and the answers would not be given orally.

STOP AND THINK

1. Why is the privilege to vote so important to the Christian citizen?

2. Why is the individual so vital in a government such as ours?

3. How could being uninformed as citizens cause the decline of our freedom?

4. List some laws of a land which would be in conflict with God's law. Can you think of any of the laws of our country which might do this?

5. Can a Christian disobey a law of the land if he feels it is unfair? Why?

6. In the light of Romans 13:1-2 would we be committing a sin against God if we run a stop sign?

7. Does the Christian have the right to seek a specific blessing from God for the leaders of the land?

8. Do you believe that peace can be brought about by prayer?

9. Using God's word as our proof, why should the Christian not look to the government for his support?

10. Discuss some of the dangers which face the American citizen today and how the Christian can help meet them.

CHAPTER XI

THE WIDOW AND THE OLDER WOMAN

Today was her anniversary, the first since the passing of her husband. The day had seemed long and quite lonely until, toward evening, she took her scrapbook and sat by the window. As the shades of the day deepened into dusk, she poured over each page, thinking . . . thinking. How long the time seemed since that terrible day when the doctor's gentle words told her that now she was alone. At first she felt she could not bear the acute pain of solitude, not when her life had been so full, so happy. Yet each hour passed into a day and each day passed into a week and soon the months had pushed behind. The wound in her heart was healing, but she knew the scar tissue would remain. Life would continue to roll on, hour after hour, day after day and what her life would consist of depended upon the will she knew must be exerted in making it a positive, rich existence. She often tried to think of time as God might look at it. When she succeeded her heart was made lighter by the realization that her best loved would have to wait only a few minutes. Then she would be ready to join him. In God's eyes it might appear just a few moments, yet she knew she would have to keep them filled for here on earth it seemed longer and she could not wait lazily for that joyous reunion! Her thoughts often drifted to the times when he had to wait for her since he was always ready first. So, in reality, she liked to feel that he again was prepared ahead of her and was only waiting for her to finish and come to meet him.

The role of widowhood is perhaps the most difficult that woman will have to accept. It carries with it the sad feeling of being separated from part of herself. When she was married, she became one flesh with her husband. When she becomes a widow, the source of love and understanding is severed and she stands alone in a world where she no longer is "first" in the heart of anyone. Certainly she is loved by her children and friends, but these have their own lives. They will include her in their love, but she no longer occupies the chief seat in anyone's life. While this feeling is desolate and painful, it will only prove fatal if fed by bitterness and self-pity. The death it produces does not affect the physical body, but the more vital spiritual life. To make this loneliness "work together for good" is the primary task of the widow after the initial shock of death has passed.

THE CHRISTIAN MUST ACCEPT DEATH AS A REALITY OF LIFE. In giving life to mankind, God includes the urge of self-preservation. It is normal to want to go on living, even though we long to know and understand the wonderful mysteries of Eternity. Yet our Creator did not intend that we should live forever. We are allotted a time upon this earth and then we must leave. This is the pattern ordained by our heavenly Father. It is natural and good when we look at it in the way He desires us to. We accept birth as the normal function of producing life in our world. Yet we fight bitterly against the acceptance of death as the termination of this life. Perhaps this is because we feel our existence is too short, too fleeting. The Bible contains many, many passages concerning the brevity of man's life. It is "a flower that fadeth and is blown away" (Psalms 103:15); "a shadow that passeth away" (Psalms 144:4); "all flesh is as grass" (James 1:10); "your life is a vapour" (James 4:14). All these point vividly to the truth that life is brief and we should not expect more. And death is the natural termination of this God-given existence. "And as it is appointed unto man once to die, but after this the judgment" (Hebrews 9:27). If we can accept birth as the way which God has chosen to bring us into this world, then we should as naturally accept death as His way of having us leave. Death is normal and only when we are ignorant of God's word does it hold terror for us. We know that "perfect love casteth out fear" (I John 4:18) and to love is to keep His commandments. Therefore if we are living in His way, death can hold no fear for us.

THE CHRISTIAN MUST FACE THE POSSIBILITY OF WIDOWHOOD. We do not like to dwell on thoughts of death yet it should not be unfamiliar in our preparation of living the Christian life. Every actuary table indicates that women outlive men by a large majority. Since this seems to be a fact of life, as Christian women we must be concerned with making our lives so secure in God that we can face the role of widowhood if and when it comes to us. Our husband is the dearest person on earth to us; he is part of our being. Yet at the core of our life should be God for He is the only non-changing thing in all our existence. The only adequate preparation for widowhood is bound up in seeking His way first and then fitting all other relationships of our life into that way. Even with this preparation, death strikes a chilling blow to the woman left behind and it will take much strength of character to use this provision to help her carry on. Only the God-centered, God-controlled life can bear the strain and stress of this most agonizing time in her life. In building a firm Christian life with her husband and children, the woman is actually storing up the necessary provisions which will enable her to meet this ordeal when it comes. To shut her eyes to the thought of being left does not take the reality from life. To refuse to accept the possibility would be to hide one's head in the sand. While a meager protection might be obtained, life in all its surrounding beauty will be concealed. Death has been passed to all and only a recognition of God and His purposes can help us fit it into the proper place in our life.

THE CHRISTIAN WIDOW MUST ACCEPT HER ALONENESS. The crushing weight of loneliness seems to engulf the woman whose husband has passed on. This perhaps is the first feeling she will experience after the initial shock. The happiness and fullness of her future life will depend upon her attitude toward this feeling. To submit to *loneliness* is tragic indeed; to utilize *aloneness* can be profitable and rewarding. One of the most precious possessions of life is that part of our being which belongs to us exclusively. This is the deep well of just ourselves; no one but God can actually occupy that place. In living a life as a wife and mother, we sometimes try to force these to come into that center-core of ourselves. But this is an artificial inhabitation and never fully satisfying. To be certain, all our loved ones must abide close to that part of us if we are to be happy; but within its portals only we and God can pass and feel natural and at home. When we are widowed, our feeling of loneliness can either make us retreat into our *alone* cell and remain there or else it will lead us there, let us abide for a time to renew our confidence in ourselves and then we will be ready to come out to the world and meet it with open heart and arms for what it shall offer us.

In living the rich life of wife and mother, we have sometimes forgotten that we are individuals in our own right. Our days are filled with thinking of others and this is as it should be. But there should be times of *aloneness* when we seek to renew our faith in ourselves and to recognize that we, too, are a person with needs and desires. The widow will have the need to seek that place within herself, to re-evaluate what she is as a person and to realize what she can be. Then she must emerge, alone but not lonely, to take her place in the world. You see, her companion within herself was the greatest comforter of all. Not only did she come to know herself better but she is closer to Him also.

THE CHRISTIAN WIDOW HAS A PLACE TO FILL IN LIFE. If the woman left is young and has children, her life of necessity will be full. Her time will not hang so heavily on her hands. This can serve a worthy purpose because physical activity is one of the best cures for emotional distress. In keeping busy serving others, the young widow can more easily make the adjustments necessary in her life. The demands on her will be greater because she must step into the role of being head of the family in addition to her already familiar capacity as mother. She will need assistance in meeting the needs of this new life and it is here that other Christians fulfill their responsibility to bear the burdens of others. Perhaps she only needs wise counsel. The elders and the older women stand ready to fill this need. It may be that she will have to have financial assistance until some arrangement can be made to provide for her family. Here again her fellow Christians must accept the opportunity of "the cup of cool water" in His name. Such acts of love and interest can do much to help the bereaved wife through this trying time.

The danger of feeling unneeded and unwanted is more prevalent if the widow is older and has no children at home. Her home and husband have been the center of her activities; now there is a great emptiness where this service once was. But the Christian widow must not retreat into a shell of self-pity and loneliness. This will engender only a bitter, unhappy life and this is not acceptable. Just because her role as a wife has been completed, she must not feel that God does not have a place for her. Sometimes in her self-interest she lets her communication with God be one-sided. A widow once told me, "I did not stop feeling useless and unloved until I realized that I must not only *talk to* God but I have to be willing to *listen,* to what He says also." Prayer is so vital to the widow and so helpful in strengthening her for what she must face. Yet a prayer-life without also reading God's word is utilizing only one aid, walking with only one crutch when you need two.

The older widow can serve in many ways. She must first make the decision to push her own feelings to the background and fill her time with a concern for others. She will have more free time to give to the Lord now. Her housework will not keep her busy and she can include service to her fellow man in her daily life. She can sew, cook, visit and counsel those who have the need. She can give time to the office work at the church, doing the many small tasks which present themselves in the routine operation of the congregation. Perhaps there is a young widow who must work and the older woman might be able to stay with her children, thus assuring they will be cared for in a godly manner. Service is a way of life and the widow can fill a valuable place in that life.

THE BALM OF HEALING FOR THE WIDOW INCLUDES MANY THINGS. Death of the husband strikes a cruel wound to the beloved wife. It seems at first that nothing can alleviate the suffering caused by the injury. Yet God in His wisdom, does not allow such a wound to remain fresh and alive. It is His natural way to let the passage of time bring the healing balm which closes the wound and eases the pain. The basic remedy used by most sorrowing women is that of tears. These are the release-valve of a pent-up heart. Women have used them to relieve the sorrow in their lives since the beginning. And God has observed their weeping, knowing and understanding the anguish which causes them to flow (Psalms 56:8 and Isaiah 38:3-5). From the sorrowing tears, woman must search deeper within herself for the faith which will restore her spiritual health. If we truly believe Romans 8:28, then faith can make us whole again. "All things work together for good to them that love God . ." And the blessed comfort of knowing that *all things* includes the death of a loved one! We cannot see how this could fit into a pattern of good for us; only time will reveal this truth to us. But it is our *faith* which will cause us to look forward and not try to go back along a way which is impossible to re-tread. Our faith will give us the courage to pick up the threads of our life and weave them into a useful garment. For it is work that brings about the most effectual healing. Association with and service for other people will hasten the healing of death's wound to our life.

MEMORY MUST HELP THE CHRISTIAN WIDOW. God has endowed mankind with the ability to remember. This is a wonderful part of the mind. It would be sad indeed if we could not bring out the precious memories of past times and dearly loved ones. These can sustain us and give a rich influence to our life. But we should always keep in mind that memories are to be kept for special times and not allowed constant exposure. We might compare them to delicate photograph negative. It contains the true likeness of the picture but if it is exposed to light for a long time, it will be useless. Memory can serve to keep the loved one close to our heart but if it is kept continuously in the forefront of our life, it will serve no worthwhile purpose. It will blind us to the present—the *now*, the *today* which we must live in. Memory is the past and as such, must play only a secondary role in living. Paul admonished us to put the past behind us and press on with the now toward the future. No one can live in the past without causing distress to himself and to others around him.

OTHER CHRISTIANS PLAY A PART IN THE LIFE OF THE WIDOW. The woman who has been left in this world has been given special attention in God's word. The relationship which fellow Christians sustain toward her will have much to do with their eternal destiny. "Pure religion and undefiled before God and the Father is this, to visit the fatherless and the widows in their affliction, and to keep himself unspotted from the world" (James 1:27). If our religion is to be acceptable to God, we must visit, or provide for, widows. This is a positive statement. There should be no misunderstanding. We are to care for them—but God has not specified *how*. It can be done in our homes, in a central home or by helping someone else care for them. But it must be done; only the way we do it is left to our discretion. There are other directions for their care given in I Timothy 5:4-16. If the widow has any children or close relatives, they are charged with her support. If she has no one to care for her, or if her family is unable to do so, the responsibility rests on the church to provide for her (Acts 6:1 and I Timothy 5:9-10). There are certain qualifications which she must fill before she can be accepted under the full support of the church. She must be at least sixty years of age and have lived a life of service and love for others. Secular history reveals that the early church had widows fitting these provisions enrolled for support. These women received their livelihood from the body of Christ and gave their lives to good works in His name. If she cannot qualify for full support of the church, then it is the responsibility of the individual Christians to relieve her needs.

THE CHRISTIAN WIDOW IS STRENGTHENED BY HOPE. All of the things which we have discussed will serve to secure a full, happy life for the widow. The passage of time may bring another mate into her life. But any remarriage is limited to God's standard. The Christian widow can marry only in the body of Christ; her new mate must also be a Christian (I Corinthians 7:39). Whatever her future life might bring, there is one other source of strength which we would mention in closing this section. This is hope. "God shall wipe away all tears . . . and there shall be no more death, neither sorrow, nor crying, neither shall there be any more pain: for the former things are passed away" (Revelation 21:4). The Christian widow holds firmly to this precious promise given by God. She lives acceptably in His sight, reaching for the fulfillment of that hope. Her mind cannot fully grasp the meaning of a land where there will be no death to shatter the heart; no sorrow to plague the mind; no parting from loved ones and no tears. She cannot understand the complete bliss of this promised land but this she knows, she wants to be there. As David said in speaking of his dead son, "He cannot return, but I can go where he is." This is the hope she clings to as she steadfastly walks in the way leading to its fulfillment.

THE OLDER WOMAN

God did not create us to live forever on this earth. As we near the end of our life span, the world says we are *old*. It seems strange that we desire to live as long as possible, yet dread growing old. Perhaps this is because we fail to understand the meaning of age and what its blessings can be. Growing old is not really just the passage of time which brings about the decline of our physical body. Growing old would seem to be more a state of mind. We are old when we can no longer open our minds to accept new thoughts, when we cease to grow in deed and concept of right. I have known people who seemed old at forty because they had shut their mind in a staid pattern of tolerating life and never reaching out to new heights, new concepts of love, new depths of feeling. On the other hand I know lovely people who are young at the physical age of seventy or eighty. Their lives mirror the beauty of their active minds—open and ready to learn something from whatever life brings their way. So it would seem that we have no need to grow old if the mind and heart is kept active and full.

AGE ONLY MAGNIFIES OUR QUALITIES. I once heard a young woman express her thoughts in this way, "I'll be so glad when I'm old, then it won't be so hard to be good and kind and sweet." How mistaken she was! Age does not bring about a change of character; it only enhances and magnifies those qualities which we possess when we are younger—the clay of the youthful life hardening with the passage of time. The shape does not change; it is firmed into a solid form for the duration of its existence. If we are impatient, grouchy and harsh at thirty, then most likely we will be even more impatient, grouchy and harsh when we reach seventy. Just as age tends to harden the arteries of the body, it also tends to solidify the traits which will either make us a joy or a terror in our old age. When we see a beautiful older woman with her kind face and white hair, we can be assured that she built that image on qualities that were developed and improved while she was much younger. If we want to be a gentle, sweet old woman, then we had better start being a gentle sweet young woman. This why it is so vital that we live each day of our lives in the righteousness pattern outlined by God. Only by a day to day preparation can we be assured of meeting His approval in the later years of our life here on earth and finally, before His throne on the day of judgment. It takes a lifetime of preparation to produce a worthy aged

Christian. P. D. Wilmeth, in his book on the Christian home, defines this time of life by saying, "Age is a state of mind, bounded on the north by resignation, on the east by memory, on the south by understanding, and on the west by service." I, too, feel that these are the best qualities of age. The boundaries must be maintained in good repair, for if one of them is either neglected or over-used, the life will not be preserved to its best advantage.

AGE COMES TO ALL WHO REMAIN UPON EARTH. Like birth and death, age is a normal process. If God allows a person to remain upon the earth, the passage of time will bring old age to him. This is a natural aspect of living and again should hold no fear for us if we are living as God has ordained. To fear old age is like being afraid to look at the view after we have trudged carefully up the rugged mountainside. Age has been compared to the top of the mountain while youth is the valley and adulthood is the mountainside. The view from the top is always better and more revealing. To want to remain young would be like limiting our view to only what can be seen in the valley around us. Only with age can we look out upon the vastness of life and under-stand more of what it is like and appreciate the depths and hues of the myriad coloring surrounding it. Robert Browning put it this way, "Grow old along with me, the best is yet to be!"

To fight age is foolish and will surely make you appear ridiculous. Millions of dollars are spent every year in America by women who are seeking the "fountain of youth." Cosmetics, facial lifts, undergarments, clothing, hair styles—in her vain attempt to remain young, the American woman spends her time and money employing these artificial supports to her ego. Growing old grace-fully should be the goal of every Christian woman. Her clothing, her manner, her very way of life will mark her as the dignified, gracious person God in-tended her to be. Nothing we can use, nothing we can do, will stop the passage of time nor cause our physical bodies to remain at the same level of preservation. To spend our valuable time in seeking the impossible is folly—both in the eyes of man and God. One unknown poet put it aptly, "When we realize, dear friend, life is a one way track, no matter how many detours, none of them will lead you back." The fountain of physical youth is a myth and search as we may, it never will be found.

WHILE THE OUTWARD DIES, THE INWARD IS RENEWED. From the moment of birth, the physical body starts its steady trudge down the road which will see it finally decline and end in decaying dust. From the fall of man, God has ordained this to be so. Physical death is part of each of us and before this termination of life, the years will bring a deterioration of the human body. As we grow older, our body is no longer vigorous and healthful as in our youth. King Solomon describes the lessening of our physical powers in Ecclesiastes 12. Our legs, our teeth, our hearing, our eyes, our strength to work—all are affected as the years press onward. We are blessed in our day by many modern technical advances which have helped the medical profession to prolong the life span. But even these "miracle" drugs and methods cannot prevent time from taking its toll on our bodies. This, too, is a natural part of life that God has prescribed for man. We can do much to help keep our bodies more healthy, but in the final reckoning, the "temple of God" will decay no matter how carefully it is cared for.

With the Christian there is a reverse process going on. While the outward body becomes more decrepit and useless, the inward part is still growing in strength. "Though our outward man perish, yet the inward man is renewed day by day" (II Corinthians 4:16). The spiritual part of our life need not fall into the decline which the physical part faces. If we look to God and keep faithfully His way for us, our inward being will be growing stronger as we move closer to the cessation of our existence on earth. This, perhaps, is what is meant by age being a state of mind. Our body might bear a weight of years, but our spirit is lifted on the wings of the eagle. Youthful vigor remains with our soul throughout eternity.

GOD HAS A PLACE FOR THE OLDER WOMAN. God recognized the value of a woman who has matured in His knowledge. Titus 2:3-5 gives the explicit instructions for the role He expects her to fill. She now has the ability and wisdom to use in teaching the younger women. Only the passage of time can bring the maturity of study and experience which enables the older woman to serve as counselor. This is true with men God instructed to be appointed elders. Knowledge alone will not bring the wisdom and maturity to equip a person to advise those who are younger. Experience of time serves its purpose in bringing such a life to ripened fruition in guiding others.

Though the older woman finds her greatest source of love and enjoyment in her family, she must not engulf it, holding it to herself and demanding all of its time and attention. She can accept the joy of the youth of her grandchildren without the responsibility attached to their care. She has a greater capacity to relax and give her thoughts to study since she is not involved with the daily activities of keeping a home. Each of the limitations upon the older woman can usually be turned into a blessing if she sets her will to it. Relieved of these physical duties, she can give more time to the exercise of her mind. No longer being charged with the physical care of children, she can serve as a close confidant and counselor to the young people around her. Whatever her lot in life, the older woman knows that she cannot "retire" from the service of the Lord. Her active duties may of necessity be curtailed but she will still seek a way to worship and serve Him. He has commanded her to be "always abounding in the work of the Lord" and to "Rejoice!" Life has been rich, full and rewarding. She is nearing the time when it will be complete. But she knows that death is only the golden key which opens the door to eternity for her. The key is almost within her reach. Soon it will be hers and she will pass through the portals leading to the fulfillment of God's promises.

SPECIAL ASSIGNMENTS

1. Prepare a lesson on God's approved way for caring for the widows and aged. Spend one class period on this.

2. Prepare a list of the aged in your congregation and set up an active program of visitation with them.

3. Have some of the children's classes make visits to the aged, taking small gifts they have made or singing for them.

STOP AND THINK

1. Why is the loss of the husband so great to the wife, using Genesis 2:24 as a basis?

2. Why do you feel death is so frightening to man?

3. In filling the role of wife and mother, why is it so necessary to remember that we are also a separate individual apart from these loved ones?

4. Why do you suppose physical labor is so beneficial in relieving emotional distress?

5. If tears are the "safety-valve" of the emotions, would there ever be a time when we should seek to stop their flow in another?

6. Discuss how sorrow can become self-pity without the widow realizing it is happening.

7. If the widow has no one to care for her and she is not sixty years of age, can the church take on her full support? If not, how can she be cared for?

8. Why do you feel it is so important to women to feel and look younger than her years? Do you feel this is justified?

9. In light of God's instructions in caring for our older people, what should the Christian's view be on government support for all our aged?

10. In carrying out the instructions in Titus 2:3-5, do you feel the older woman should seek out the younger or wait until she herself is sought out for advice? Why?

CHAPTER XII

THE TEENAGE GIRL

The living room was quiet. The mother and father sat deep in thought. Mother was hiding her emotions behind rapidly moving needles fashioning a sweater. Father had the newspaper before his face but his eyes did not read the words nor did his mind comprehend their meaning. Upstairs their daughter was dressing in preparation for her first date! The door bell rang and caused both parents to react with a visible start. Father arose and went to answer it. When he swung it open, there stood a fine looking young man—a bit nervous, but nevertheless quite nice. Inviting him to come in, the father went before him back to the living room. After speaking to the mother, the boy sat on the corner of the couch. The mother went to the stairs and calling gently, she told her daughter her date had arrived. Soon the young girl appeared on the steps and as she came down them, the mother felt she had never seen such regal bearing. Her thoughts went back just a few hours ago when this same queenly young lady would stumble over her feet in descending these exact stairs. The young woman took the arm of the boy and together they left for their big evening.

The thoughts of both parents were at the same time sad and yet joyful. Their daughter had come to them through God's love and they had tried to bring her up in the way which He deemed right. Now she was a teenager—beginning the most trying years of life. They were so full of love for her and they wanted only what was best for her. Yet they knew they could not rely on their own wisdom. It was not sufficient. Together they sat on the couch and joined their hearts in prayer to God. This was the source of their strength in the past and they knew they would rely on it to see their precious child through the dangerous years and into a full, happy adult life.

The teenage girl is a special being all her own. Never before has she presented the characteristics which have suddenly ripened in her life. And probably never again will these qualities be exhibited in exactly the same way. She is reaching out to the world one minute—eager to gain all it can offer. The next minute she draws back into her own private shell—rejecting any touch of companionship. She will eat a combination of foods which might turn the stomach of her parents and then refuse to dine upon steak and salad. She is anguished in turn about the following: boys, clothing, boys, food, boys, her figure and boys again. Lest we give the impression that the male sex plays too important part in her interests, let us look at another side of her. She is happy when deeply involved in discussion with her girl friends and while this discussion sometimes includes those creatures with the short hair and long pants, it also touches upon subjects which her parents feel are amazingly mature. She can serve hours as a "candy-striper" volunteer at the hospital, patiently carrying trays and massaging bedsore backs and reading endless stories to the young patients. Yet she can feel "overtired" after making one bed and hanging up a skirt and blouse.

Her life is centered around extremes. Everything is *too* little, *too* big, *too* sad, *too* happy. Everything is just *too* much! She tends to clumsiness but when the occasion demands, she can bear herself like the regal being she feels she is. She will either talk too much or else will not communicate at all. Her emotions are either of joyous love or darkest hate. She is either up or down. There seems to be no middle ground for her. Her personality is like quicksilver, slipping from one facet to another without one realizing where the first went. She is lovable and loving. She will respect you if your actions deserve it and will let you know when they do not command her admiration. She needs your love. She needs your respect. She needs your care. Whatever she is, whatever qualities she possesses, whatever she does—she is your daughter. God has given her to you as a heritage and there are no words adequate to express your love for His gift.

The relationship between teenage daughter and her parents is not always an easy one. These are the years when most of our children are lost to the church, and sometimes even to society. It is vital, therefore, that we look into both sides and by seeking God's help, find the way that will bring happiness in this life and in eternity also. Responsibilities fall on both parties and our study will include the duties of each.

EACH TEENAGE DAUGHTER HAS THE RIGHT TO BE CARED FOR. In entrusting this child to us, God has enjoined us to provide for her material needs. She has the right to expect that we will give her a home, food, clothing and the other material provisions necessary to exist. What these will be, of course, depends upon our financial ability. She has the right to expect a home, but she must be satisfied with that which is provided. As parents we should be willing to sacrifice posessions for ourselves to make certain that our children are adequately supplied. I remember my own mother owning only one good dress and wearing that for two or three years in order that my sisters and I could have school clothes, not elaborate but sufficient for the need. My father wore the same suit until the pants were so thin and shiny it was dangerous to bend over. There were times when they did not put very much on their own plates until they were certain we had eaten enough. This was done in such a way that we children were not aware they were doing without. Only in looking back can we see the personal sacrifices made so that we could have enough to eat and adequate clothing. At the time I felt we were poor but the maturity of years has taught me we were indeed wealthy to have had such parents. Our daughter should have the same attitude from us. We will not try to give her more than is good for her but she will be lovingly cared for to the best of our abilities.

THE TEENAGE GIRL HAS THE RIGHT TO EXPECT LOVE. If we realize that God gave us this child, then we will love her. Every child has the need to be loved for herself alone, not for what she can do. This young girl should be granted the privilege of the right kind of love—a love which will foster her growth both physically and spiritually. We cannot expect her to have the capacity to love others unless she has experienced that love herself. This is the human way. "We love him, because he first loved us" (I John 4:19). The young girl who has not known the love of good parents and a kind home cannot offer the proper affection to others. We will not be guilty of holding our love as a premium for her obedience. For if she does disobey, we will still love her just as God loved us and sent His Son while we were *yet in our sins.* Our love is constant, firm and constructive. It will be there when she needs it; it will support her when she is weak; and it will help her choose the right way to go.

THE TEENAGE GIRL HAS A RIGHT TO EXPECT RESPECT AND FAIRNESS. She is a human being and as such, has her own qualities which must be judged from the standpoint of environment, association and knowledge. We must respect her for what she is, not for what we would like to make of her. She has the prerogative of knowing that we will accept her on her own merits and not compare her to some other young person of her own family or in the family of a friend. We must see her own capabilities and do all that we can to help her develop them. But we will not be guilty of "pushing" her into a mold which does not suit her abilities. We will respect her person, not demanding too much of her. This will be difficult since she is now a young woman and as mothers, we might be prone to let her shoulder too many of our own responsibilities. She will have her own duties and will fulfill them but she is not our "assistant" housekeeper and we will respect her in this physical work. We will see to it that she has some privacy—this too she has the right to expect. Everyone needs time alone to get to know oneself better. We will arrange our schedule so that she may seek privacy and we will respect this need. Her mail, her phone calls, her diary, her personal belongings?—these will merit our deference. There may be a time when we deem it necessary to intrude upon these privacies but even then we will try to do it after counseling with her and gaining her approval if at all possible.

THE TEENAGE GIRL HAS THE RIGHT TO EXPECT DISCIPLINE. The great blot on our American youth today is juvenile delinquency. The courts of our country are filled with the unsavory actions of these unfortunate young people. Most psychologists agree that the youth who gets into trouble with the authorities does so because he has never been taught to respect authority at home. Discipline is the security of these children. We must set the bounds within which we expect our children to live. They must *know* these boundaries and act accordingly. Our discipline should be fair, firm and administered with love and for the proper reason—to teach the child. The purpose of parental discipline is to foster self-discipline in the youth. This is the goal which we strive for because we will not always be on hand to make the decision for them. They must learn to choose the right for themselves and our discipline will be aimed at that end. The wise proverb tells us to "train up" our children. This is an active, disciplined teaching program. In it they will find security for a rich, happy life and in the end, it will provide the basis for acceptance in heaven.

THE TEENAGE GIRL HAS A RIGHT TO BOTH A FATHER AND A MOTHER. The normal pattern for the home provides a father, a mother and children. Of course, we realize that all these components are not always present, either by reason of death or some other thing. But we will be speaking of the normal situation where both parents are available. Some people mistakenly think the sex of the child determines whether it should receive more attention from the father or the mother. The son needs both the mother and the father. And even more important, the teenage daughter needs the love and attention of her father, as well as her mother. Judge Tatum of Nashville, Tennessee, once stated that the biggest majority of teenage girls who passed through his courts did not have the proper attention from their father. The young girl needs the strength of the head of the family to let her recognize her own place in God's pattern. She will learn how to love properly from the influence of his life and attitude toward his family. He must give her the wonderful feeling that he notices her and that he loves her and is pleased with her. He should compliment her and help her find her proper place in life. The young girls need their mothers also. She will be the confidant, the crying towel, the steady support, the source of information. She will fill all these roles with God-given wisdom and courage, knowing that this young girl, like the tender rosebud, is being led toward the blossoming of her life. Nothing should be done to mar and destroy that tender life.

THE TEENAGE GIRL HAS THE RIGHT TO EXPECT SPIRITUAL GUIDANCE. If the parents are not willing to feed the spiritual side of their children as well as the physical, they should never bring them into the world. The child who is nourished physically and neglected spiritually will present a warped life to the world. As Christians, God has commanded that we train our children in His way. We have an excellent example of this in young Timothy, who was taught so ably by his mother and grandmother. This guidance can be given by positive teaching and also by the influence of godly lives. The combination of these serve to instruct our children in spiritual growth. Without the proper nourishment, the soul of the child will not be prepared to meet God. How terrible if our daughter faced us in the judgment saying, "But you didn't tell me what to do and your life never showed the way I should go!" Spiritual guidance and training during the teen years will mold our young daughter into the maturity of Christian womanhood, prepared to accept the responsibilties of being a wife and mother herself. This training will include a knowledge of her physical being and the God-given purposes it serves. This young girl will understand that her body is a worthy instrument if used as God directs. She will learn her proper position in relation to man. When she passes the teen years, her life will be ready to assume its obligations and privileges because she has a close and intimate knowledge of her Maker and what He expects of her. Her parents have seen to that.

THE PARENTS HAVE THE RIGHT TO EXPECT THEIR DAUGHTER TO RETURN THEIR AFFECTION. Nothing is more unsatisfactory than a one-sided relationship. Many teenage daughters take it as their due to have the love of their parents. Yet they feel no obligation nor urge to return even a part of that affection. Love to be perfected, must be returned, thus forming a circle. Love flows to love and then back again in a never-ceasing stream. The bond between parent and child should be close and sure, with parent showing devotion to child and then child returning that tenderness of heart. Our teenagers should understand just how much that kind word or loving deed means to their folks. Mother and father are willing to give abundantly; surely it is not asking too much for the daughter to reciprocate with a show of love.

THE PARENTS HAVE A RIGHT TO RECEIVE APPRECIATION FOR THE MATERIAL BLESSINGS THEY PROVIDE. No parent would ever invoke this right. It is not their nature. They give the care necessary because they love their child and do not expect her to be constantly thanking them. Yet it is the moral duty of that daughter to show her appreciation for the possessions and loving care she is being given. This is a characteristic exhibited by Paul in II Thessalonians 1:3 and is worthy of being emulated in our life. Modern parents shower material possessions upon their children to the extent that the child begins to accept them as his normal lot. Perhaps they never realize the sacrificial attitude behind this giving. The Christian teenager will develop an insight of gratitude for the kindness shown and be able to prove his appreciation by his good behavior and kind actions toward others.

THE PARENTS HAVE A RIGHT TO EXPECT THE RESPECT OF THEIR DAUGHTER. This would have to be qualified by stating, the right is there if their lives command the respect. Just being a parent does not automatically make us deserving of the admiration of our children. Teenagers are quick to see if we do not measure up to the standards we have set for them. They think logically and come up with the answer that if the standard is not acceptable for mother and father, why should they be expected to follow it. But disrespect for their elders is altogether too common among our teenagers today, even among Christian young people. We should first earn their respect and having lived in such a way as to deserve it, we must see to it that our child is taught to show the proper attitude toward us and other adults. The teaching starts at an earlier age than the teen years though and may come too late if we wait until then.

THE PARENTS HAVE THE RIGHT TO OBEDIENCE FROM THEIR DAUGHTER. Discipline of the child is God-expected and God-approved. The Christian parent begins this vital training at an early age and thus can expect obedience from their child. If we give them no discipline, we have withheld security from them. To reach the precarious teen years without security would be frightening indeed. Obedience is the beautiful characteristic which makes man walk acceptably before God. This is the key to the relationship of the creature and the Creator. One gives the law; it is for the other to obey. I John 5:2 tells us "by this we know that we love God, when we keep his commandments." If this is the criteria by which our love for God is judged, then it can aptly be used in the parent-child relationship. If the chid loves his parents, he will obey them. God has given them a direct command to do this in Colossians 3:20, "Children, obey your parents in all things: for this is well pleasing unto the Lord." This same command is given in Ephesians 6:1. Thus disobedience of one's parents not only brings sorrow to the heart of that loved one, but it does the same to the heavenly Father.

These "rights" spoken of do not cover all the areas of this relationship. They have given us just an insight into some of the misunderstandings which can bring so much anguish between teenage daughter and loving parents. There are many scriptures given to both sides in this affiliation of love. We shall not try to list them all. There are many worthwhile books printed which can be of help to both daughter and parents. These should be sought and utilized. Many times the child can gain more from an outsider in looking at her problems and understanding they are not so different from those of thousands of other girls her age. The parents should feel no jealousy if she seeks help in either a book or from the counsel of another person. By the same token the parents should seek guidance in a study of God's word, using the many books written on the teen years, and asking advice from some older parent who has brought children safely through these years.

I am going to close this study with two statements written from different viewpoints. I have two teenage daughters and one will be in those magical, trying years on her next birthday. I may by no means be an expert but I have had a little experience. From this, the following words are penned:

THOUGHTS OF A TEENAGE GIRL

"I don't really know *who* I am. Sure I know my name and my family background, but I really don't know *me* yet. I know what I want to be, though and I know a lot about what can make me reach that goal. First, I want to be loved and understood by my mother and father. I have funny ideas sometimes and I act in silly ways and even unkind ways, which I don't really want to be doing. But I wish my parents could look beneath that outer me and see that my heart is not really like that.

I want to be friendly and have friends. Why is it that when I meet someone I really admire and respect, I act in such a way as to make them not like me? Maybe I am trying to hide my feeling of insecurity by putting on this silly behaviour. Sometimes I'm too sincere in dealing with my friends. I tell them exactly what I think and even though it's the truth, it would have been kinder to keep my mouth shut. I want to be loyal and have a lot of friends but it seems like I wind up pleasing just a few and hurting others. Will I ever have the easy-going, poised relationship with other people that I want so badly?

I want to be popular; I want to be liked by the boys and the girls, and even my teachers! How can I achieve this? Do I try too hard or not hard enough? I want to have the high Christian ideals which my parents have taught me from God's word, but I wonder if they realize how difficult it is to be alone in a crowd that does not understand why I cannot participate in their idea of fun. I don't really want to do the things they do, but I would so like to be a part of the crowd. I wish it were possible to be accepted and still not conform to their standards. How can I live the Christian life without appearing the prude or the "square" to my friends? Oh, I wish I knew the answer! I want to date good, clean boys and enjoy their company. How do I make them like me for what I am and not expect something from me which I cannot give? How do I make that cute boy in history class *really* look at me? Sure he sees me every day but only as a fixture of the room. Do I dare to be a little forward? I wonder if mother could help if I asked her? Maybe dad would be the one to ask. I wonder what boys really want girls to be like. He could tell me that.

I want to marry some day. I hope he's a Christian and if I go to a Christian college, surely I'll find the one for me. How will I know he is the one? Will there be some special emotion like electricity when he's around? What if I don't recognize the right one? Or worse yet, what if he doesn't recognize me? I hope I am the kind of wife and mother that will bring only good to my family. What am I doing in life? Am I going the right way? Who am I? Where do I go to find the answers? Can't someone help me?"

THOUGHTS OF A CHRISTIAN MOTHER

"Daughter of my heart, how can I help you find out who you are when I have not yet learned all about myself? But maybe I can let you see yourself from my viewpoint and this will help you know that you are a real person, loved and cherished. You came to us as a gift from God, brought about by the love of your father and I, and nurtured in the closeness of our family circle. So tiny and dear, yet a separate person even then. Now you are a teenager. The time has passed so swiftly and you stand before me a young woman. Your body shows the maturity with which God has endowed womankind. Your mind is beginning to show that it, too, is growing in the wonderful knowledge of life, of God and of the mysteries which make themselves known at your age. We do see beyond the exterior you present to the world and what we see brings a great swell of pride to our hearts.

We see the friendliness which you show to others, especially to the unlovely and unloved people you meet. This is a quality you don't recognize in yourself but we see it. Surely, you act foolishly at times but life for you can seem foolish and full of hilarity. Your actions only prove you to be a normal young girl, experiencing the first real knowledge of life at its best.

Your popularity is the kind which we approve—not the woman-of-the-world variety, but the wonderful wholesome respect of your girl friends; the shy, awkward gallantry of the young boys we see you greet; and we know how your teachers feel that you are special. You *are* popular and the secret of your popularity is that you don't know it exists!

We have earnestly tried to give you the best standard available—the word of God. We know our own lives fail to be the best example at times, but surely you are mature enough to see the love and desires for right beneath our clumsy actions. Our prayers have been not only for your physical health but that you might mature spiritually and thus prepare yourself adequately to become the wonderful wife and mother we know you can be. We only pray that God, in His providence, is preparing a good, clean boy to be your husband and the father of your children. Surely somewhere there are parents of a son who feel the same way we do about God and His way. That boy, we pray, will be the one you meet, date, fall in love with and marry. You will have our blessings and our prayers for a long, full, happy life together.

There is so much I want for you, love of my heart, but most of all I want you to be the mature Christian woman, pleasing in the eyes of God and the world. I can do a great deal to bring this to fruition and with God's help, I will."

SPECIAL ASSIGNMENTS

1. Have someone use a concordance and make a chart of all the scriptures relating to the training of children.

2. Prepare a list of church activities which can utilize our teenage girls. See about getting a program of work started for them.

3. Have a teacher of the teenage girls in your congregation give a special report on the characteristics, problems and blessings of this wonderful group.

STOP AND THINK

1. Why are the teen years so tempestuous and dangerous to our youth?

2. Discuss some of the better ways to discipline a teenager.

3. Why do you feel it is so important that a girl have the proper father-daughter relationship?

4. How far should the parent go in letting the teenager keep "secrets?" How can you instill the confidence of yourself in that child?

5. Should teenagers expect pay for performing household chores? Discuss the pros and cons of allowances.

6. Do you feel the parents should "force" the teenager to attend worship if they do not want to? Why?

7. How can we best bring about self-discipline in our children?

8. Discuss early dating and pushing our children into social situations of life before they are ready. What are the dangers in doing this?

9. Do you feel girls should have positive teaching regarding sex, their physical bodies and a proper attitude toward both? Whose responsibility is this teaching?

10. List some of the ways we can provide clean, wholesome recreation for our young people.

CHAPTER XIII

THE COMPLETE PERSONALITY

Each of the preceeding chapters has dealt with a particular role in life which most women will fill. Most of these dealt with our relationship either with God or with our fellow man. It is necessary for us to study these because we do not live to ourselves in this world and only by making the most of our associations with those around will we secure the best life, the abundant life promised by Christ in John 10:10. But in order to make that life complete and rewarding, we must also look to ourself. Until we have learned to live at peace with our own personality, then we cannot be fully successful in living with others. Many woman go through their whole life without ever finding that harmony within themselves. These are the lives marked by mental illness, broken homes, juvenile problems and the deepest of human miseries. God did not intend for us to live this way. He sent His Son that we might have a rich happy existence on this earth and finally, a home with Him throughout eternity. But it is up to the individual to seek that life and to incorporate the qualities necessary into their pattern of living. God will not force this life upon us, but He will give us help in finding it.

THE WORTH OF THE REAL ME. The individual has always been important to God. He created man and woman as individuals, giving them separate characteristics and areas of work. Each had a great worth and none other could fill their exact place. Down through time this has remained true. It is the influence of the separate beings in this world which spreads as a chain reaction, bringing about good and evil. To lump people together as a class would be inaccurate in the truest sense of the word because that lump consists of many single units, each differing in attitude and character. In the parable of the talents, Christ teaches that each person is given some ability. None had to start with absolutely nothing. This should comfort our hearts when we feel that we are useless and of no value to anyone. "I am troubled: I am bowed down greatly; I go mourning all the day long" (Psalms 38:6). This seems to be a common attitude many women take, not realizing their self-worth.

Maybe the reason lies within the service of woman's daily life. She is so absorbed by her family and friends that she does not realize she exists as a separate being. She is pulled in all directions and when these tuggings bring her to a state of depression, she has no place to retreat to find herself again. In her wonderful book, *Gift from the Sea*, Ann Lindbergh compares woman to a water pitcher. She is expected to spill her value to all around her, a constant emptying of herself. But the pitcher cannot always remain full and of necessity, she must withdraw and refill her life so that she again may go around pouring of herself to others. Mrs. Lindbergh suggests that a partial answer lies in woman seeking a time to be alone, to know herself, and to replenish her mind and heart through study, reading and thought. Then she can again take her place, refreshed and confident.

Another comparison used by Mrs. Lindbergh is that woman should be like the axis of a wheel which remains still and stationary while the spokes of life revolve around her. This stillness, this value of self proves to be the steadying influence in a world of constant worry, hurry and changing problems. If she lets herself begin to revolve with the spokes, her value is diminished and her services unsatisfactory. The secret lies in valuing oneself properly and remaining calm in the center of the activity, holding it together and keeping it on the right path.

LIVING WITH THE REAL ME. I am so grateful that God is not going to judge me in comparison with someone else. There are so many worthy women in the church today and when I measure myself by their standards, I feel quite inadequate. While I admire these talents and may even try to emulate their qualities, God does not expect that from me which I am not capable of giving. This is a comforting thought and one that helps me accept myself. I have my *own* abilities, my own worthwhile characteristics. I must learn to use them properly so that they might be increased. I also have my shortcomings and failures. I must recognize these and with God's help, overcome them. But above all I must accept both abilities and failures and learn to live with *me*. If I must compare myself with someone, it should be only with the *me* of the past. Self-degradation is not worthy of the Christian. Surely if we were loved enough to be redeemed by the blood of God's Son, then we cannot be worthless. We learn to live with others despite their faults; just as surely we must learn to live with and accept ourselves. Until we do, we will live in the turmoil of constant self-condemnation. Depression will dog our footsteps and tears will flow unceasingly. Like David, let us say, "I thought on my ways, and turned my feet unto thy testimonies" (Psalms 119:59). Certainly we have sins and failures, but only by dwelling in them and on them will they separate us from God. Recognizing them, we shall turn our feet into His path and seek His guidance to keep us there.

HAPPINESS IS FOUND WITHIN. Contrary to popular thought, true happiness cannot be found in any *thing*, any *place*, or any *other person*. The things we possess might add to our enjoyment of life, but they alone will not insure happiness. We may delight in living in a special place, perhaps the mountains, the shore, the city or the country. But there is no place in all the world that can alone bring you happiness. Being with certain people brings certain satisfaction to us but another person cannot assure us of happiness. Why? Because it is within our selves to utilize all these to either bring us joy or dissatisfaction. I may desire a certain possession with great earnestness. It becomes almost a fixation in my heart but when it is achieved, I feel the anticipation was more enriching than the actual possession. Perhaps I long to live in a certain city. I desire this so passionately I begin to think that it is almost

Utopia and if I did live there, life would be perfect. So I move there. What do I find? The problems of life remain much the same regardless of where they are placed geographically. Then we meet that certain someone and we know he is the one. If only he returns our affection—if only he will love me and ask me to marry him! Life would be a fairy castle of dreams—if only! So he does respond; he does seek my hand; we are married. Is life exactly the dream I had thought? No. The answer lies within my own limitations of using the things which come my way. True happiness is found when we learn to utilize the elements around us, no matter what they are. This reveals why the self-centered woman living in the midst of plenty can still be unhappy. It also tells us how the selfless woman abiding in the tiny cottage can be blissfully content.

No thing, no place, no human being can *make* us happy. We have to do that ourselves. Happiness is acquired through the senses we use to perceive the world—touch, smell, feel, taste, sight. We either like or dislike something through one of these avenues. God gave us these senses to make us aware of the world around us and in using them joyfully and gratefully, we can bring happiness and contentment. If one or more of these senses were lacking, then we would have more limitation in achieving happiness. But in whatever remains, we can still find a measure of joyfulness. Helen Keller is a good example of this. Blind and deaf, she has made good usage of what she did have. She once told a group, "Yes, I am blind and I cannot hear, But God left me the glorious ability and desire to soar." She used the faculties remaining to soar to heights the world thought impossible for one so handicapped. Happiness is inseparably linked with contentment, and contentment can be found anywhere geographically and economically. Paul knew this and he also taught us that it does not come automatically; it has to be learned. "I have learned, in whatsoever state I am, therein to be content" (Philippians 4:11).

THE COMPLETE PERSONALITY OF THE CHRISTIAN WOMAN. What is the complete personality of a Christian woman? Has God given us the qualities which we should possess to be a whole person? The answer to the first question cannot be given in just one sentence. The complete personality involves many things and cannot be summed up in a short statement. But the answer to the second question is "Yes" and this is why we don't have to rely on earthly wisdom to guide us. God knows our needs and He has given us adequate instructions which encompass the whole sphere of our being. Using His guide, we no longer need to worry and wonder; let us be doing!

There are three passages of scripture which we will be using in studying the traits which we must possess to be complete in God's sight. These are Galatians 5:22-24; Colossians 3-12-14; and II Peter 1:5-9. We will not quote these here, nor will we make a full study of each characteristic given. We will be selecting several of these attributes for our study, not because they are necessarily the most important, but for the value which we might gain from thinking on them.

FAITH IS THE FOUNDATION OF THE COMPLETE LIFE. "Without faith, it is impossible to please God . . ." (Hebrews 11:6). This is the foundation stone of the Christian life. If we do not believe that Jesus is the Son of God; that He came to earth and died for our sins; and that He rose triumphant from the grave, then we have no basis for our religion. How do we get that faith? Is it given us through some mysterious way which only we can feel? Romans 10:17 answers this for us. We have faith through a knowledge of God's word, believing what it says, and obeying its commands. Until we have this we cannot begin to add the other virtues to our life and expect them to serve us well. Faith might be compared to an adhesive—it is what helps us keep the other virtues tightly in our lives. It is powerful, because its source is powerful. To neglect the use and increase of our faith, is to turn our back on God's power to save us.

LOVE IS THE OUTSTANDING QUALITY OF THE CHRISTIAN. The other qualities we possess are rendered worthless if they are not tempered with love. This is the conspicious "something" which marks the Christian as different from the world. A study of the Love Chapter, I Corinthians 13, reveals that this is to be desired above all else. Faith is precious and necessary; hope is supporting and essential; but love is eternal and to love is to be like God. In heaven the Christian's faith will be made sight and our hope will become a reality. They will then cease to exist, but love will not become extinct. It will reign in the presence of God forever and ever, exemplified by both the Creator and the created.

Sir Walter Scott wrote, "Love's the gift which God has given to man alone beneath the heaven . . . It is the secret sympathy, the silver link, the silken tie, which heart to heart and mind to mind, in body and in soul can bind." This excellence of character is the endowment of a God who loved His children so much that He desired that they, too, could possess one of His own qualities. When we love, we are like God (I John 4:7).

Love is the motivating force which will lead us to obey God (I John 5:3) and will cause us to do good to all those we meet, friend and foe alike. Love is not a passive emotion; it is an activating element in our lives. Love is *giving;* love is *doing.* "For God so loved the world He gave His only begotten son . ." (John 3:16). If we say we love, and yet *do* not we are deluding ourselves. Every phase of the Christian woman's life must be arrayed in this quality. Her words, her deeds, everything about her life will be softened and guided by love. Colossians 3:14 calls it the "bond of perfectness." If we seek to be perfect in the eyes of God, this will be the dominant characteristic of our life.

THE CHRISTIAN WOMAN MUST NOT WORRY. The command not to worry is just as positive as the command to be baptized. "In nothing be anxious; but in everything by prayer and supplication with thanksgiving let your request be made known unto God. And the peace of God, which passeth all understanding, shall keep your hearts and minds through Christ Jesus"

(Philippians 4:6-7). There can be no mistaking the point in this. We are not to worry about *anything!* After all, there has never been anything accomplished by worry. It does not breed solutions; it only engenders despair and further anxiety. Our problem should be faced honestly. If we do something positive toward solving it, then let's do that, not worry. If there is absolutely nothing which we can do to help the situation, then hand the problem to God. In either case, worry will waste time, energy and effort. "Commit thy works unto the Lord, and thy thoughts shall be established" (Proverbs 16:3). "Cast your care upon him; for he careth for you" (I Peter 5:6). "Cast thy burden upon the Lord and he shall sustain thee: he shall never suffer the righteous to be moved" (Psalms 55:22). In recent years some manufacturer put a "Worry Bird" on the market. The theory behind it stated that you need not worry, let the bird do it for you. This is foolishness, we understand, yet thousands of these little statues were sold. The Christian does not have to rely upon a "worry bird" or even upon himself; God stands ready to accept the burdens we pass to Him. How many needless heavy loads we carry when we could so easily share it with Him. He will not leave us nor forsake us (Hebrews 13:5). How comforting to to know our concern is His! We need only seek His help.

THE CHRISTIAN WOMAN IS GENTLE AND KIND. Poets and authors have written thousands, yea millions of words concerning the gentleness of womankind. She has been exalted for these attributes more than any others. She was satisfied to live within those protective boundaries of life for hundreds of years. Then all at once she began to push against them, demanding "equal" rights with man. I do not question the "rights" she desired, but I severely censure the masculine characteristics she took to herself when she gained those rights. Look back just a generation or two and see how our women today compare in gentleness and kindness with those sisters of yesteryear. Harsh voices, mannish attire, dominant tendencies—too many times this is the American woman today. The Christian woman must not let these traits become a part of her life. She will be feminine, as God intended her to be from the beginning. And being feminine includes the gentlenss of demeanor and kindness of word and deed which exemplified the woman in Proverbs 31. Gentleness will help us meet the needs of those we love for this will give us an insight into their lives. It has been said that "gentleness is the eyeglass through which we understand others."

THE CHRISTIAN WOMAN WILL BE PATIENT. Perhaps no other quality is needed so badly by the Christian woman today. We are impatient with ourselves; we are impatient with our husbands; we are impatient with our children; we are impatient with fellow Christians; we are impatient with the world. The reasons for this are varied, but one of the most prevalent seems to be the rush, rush pace of the whole universe. We have jet planes which can take us across the nation in a matter of minutes; rocket ships are being developed to whisk man off into space. The automobile is being manufactured so that it will go faster and faster. Time seems to be on a giddy merry-go-round and we can't seem to slow it down. We have limited time to accomplish what needs to be done and we become impatient with anything or anybody which might get in our way.

Patience is a God-commanded virtue. "In your patience, possess ye your souls" (Luke 21:19). Quite a reward is placed on being long-suffering. In fact, our very souls depend upon it. "That we through patience and comfort of the scriptures might have hope" (Romans 15:4). Here forbearance is put on an equal scale with the comfort we gain from the Bible. "Knowing this, that the trying of your faith worketh patience. But let patience have her perfect work, that ye may be perfect, and entire, wanting nothing" (James 1:3). A complete personality? Here James says it cannot be gained without patience.

We will endure in trying to reach those out of Christ, understanding that they are not in the blessed light of the truth and it is not easy for them to do what is right. Our forebearance will include the lukewarm Christian. If we are to be spiritual, it is our duty to restore that one (Galatians 6:1) and patience will be foremost in our association with them. We will be patient with ourselves as we try to grow in spiritual maturity. Recognizing our shortcomings. we will press closer to God and be more lenient with our failures. When the bad times come, we will accept our lot with tolerance, knowing that "all things work together for good."

THE CHRISTIAN WOMAN WILL SEEK THE BEAUTY IN LIFE. Because we are so involved in housework, babies, PTA and homework, it is not always easy for us to see the beauty of life all around us. Yet it is there and as Christians, we should be aware of all that God has provided for our welfare and enjoyment. Keats, the poet, wrote, "A thing of beauty is a joy forever; its loveliness increases; it can never pass into nothingness." And since "beauty is in the eye of the beholder" we can view the world in such a way as to seek out that which is lovely. Bovee stated, "To cultivate the sense of the beautiful is one of the most effectual ways of cultivating an appreciation of the divine goodness."

There is beauty in a home well kept. The sense of self-satisfaction which comes from dusting the furniture so that the wood gleams can seldom be achieved elsewhere. Or what about the good, clean feeling of having completed an ironing. There the clothes are hanging so sweet smelling and smooth. Beauty to the eye and to the touch. And the fragrance of something cooking. Beauty to the sense of smell. There are so many things which present loveliness all around us but maybe because they are so routine, they are lost on our senses.

I decided to make a test to see just how much beauty I can see from where I am sitting writing these words. Directly before me, of course, is my typewriter. Can there be beauty there? I think so—beauty in the most utilitarian sense. How could I ever finish without the precision tool at my disposal. I lift my eyes and before me is a west window. Crisp, white curtains hang as a frame to the scene outside. My eyes fall on the hills in the distance with the graceful curve of the ski jump perched on the crest of one. Right now the trees seem barren yet still reaching upward to heaven. There is a small lake at the foot of our back yard. It is frozen at the present time, all white and glistening. Over on the other side, at the base of the hills I can see the neat homes and yards. Bringing my vision back into my immediate surroundings, I look to the left. There on the chest is an aged water pitcher and bowl set. There are minute cracks in it yet its form is graceful and enchanting, more so because it was a gift from my husband. Even the chest on which it sits catches my eye. The maple graining is gleaming and mellow. Turning my head I look at the bed covered by a neat white spread. At the foot lies the knitted and embroidered afghan so patiently collaborated on by my mother and me. On the other side is the rocking chair I sit in to read my Bible before retiring. Beside it is the table which holds several books—the Bible, *Gift from the Sea*, *Try Giving Yourself Away*, and *Daughters of Eve*. I have paused for a moment and read this last paragraph. How many things of beauty do I have surrounding me in just this one room and the view from its window! And think, there are other rooms in the house and outside, waits the world!

There is beauty in good books, in preparing a Bible lesson, in fine music, and masterpieces of art. There is beauty in being a wife and a mother. There is beauty in the life and body of a child. Nowhere can we look that we do not see beauty. But above all, there is beauty in God and this we seek most earnestly. "One thing have I desired of the Lord, that will I seek after; that I may dwell in the house of the Lord all the days of my life; to behold the beauty of the Lord, and to inquire in his temple" (Psalms 27:4).

All of the qualities given in our three texts cannot be discussed here but the Christian woman will be endeavoring to make each of them an integral part of her life. She is preparing now for that home of perfection and she will not be ready if she is not diligent in bringing forth the fruits of an acceptable, complete life.

SPECIAL ASSIGNMENTS

1. Using the three texts given in the beginning of this chapter, have the members each take one of the Christian characteristics listed and give a short discussion on it.

2. Ask each member to "seek the beauty" of things around them. See if they will not list some of those lovely things which they might see from one special place (in their home, sitting in the car, in the classroom, etc.).

3. Have each member select a project of making something beautiful (cooking, sewing, painting, scrapbook, etc.) and take these to the aged or ill of the congregation.

STOP AND THINK

1. Where is the best mirror for looking at our personality?

2. What do you feel is meant by the "abundant life" in John 10:10?

3. Why is God so interesed in the individual?

4. Discuss the dangers in self-condemnation. Scripture proof?

5. Discuss the dangers in self-righteousness. Scripture proof?

6. Do you feel that we should seek time to ourselves, apart from our husband and children? Why?

7. Why cannot things and people make us happy?

8. Discuss some of the beauties of life which can be experienced through the five senses which God gave us.

9. Why is love greater than either faith or hope?

10. Do you feel worry is a sin? Why? How can it be conquered?

EPILOGUE

We have come to the close of this series of lessons. As I stated in my Foreword, it is my prayerful hope that they might be used with value to you and in Glory to God. It sometimes seems an impossible task-this living the Christian life. Yet we know that it is not, and through Christ we can do all things. His strength can be our strength and we can rely on His wisdom. If we really want to make these changes in our life, we can do it. I would like to close by sharing with you the following from *Words to Live By* by Wilfred A. Peterson.

THE ART OF CHANGING YOURSELF

Man alone, of all the creatures of earth, can change his own pattern. Man alone is architect of his destiny.

William James declared that the greatest revolution in his generation was the discovery that human beings, by changing the inner attitudes of their minds, can change the other aspects of their lives.

History and literature are full of examples of the miracle of inner change. Do you know the Persian story of the hunchback prince who became straight and tall by standing each day before a statue of himself made straight?

Change requires the substituting of new habits for old. You mold your character and future by your thoughts and acts.

Change can be advanced by associating with those with whom you can walk among the stars.

Change can be inspired by selecting your own spiritual ancestors from among the great of all the ages. You can practice the kindliness of Lincoln, the devotion of Schweitzer, the vision of Franklin.

Change can be achieved by changing your environment. Let go of the lower things and reach for the higher. Surround yourself with the best in books, music and art.

Change can be accomplished most of all through the power of prayer, because with God all things are possible.

Let us each search our hearts and see if there is not too much of "Martha" in us. Then determine that with the help of God and His word, from now on we can be called "Mary."

Marge Green

NOTES: